"Cut over that wa... o chase him around the ot...

Joe cut his bike left, pressing up over the top of a ten-foot-high hill. At the top of the hill, two tree trunks suddenly appeared out of the fog right in front of Joe.

Frank put on a final burst of speed with his bike and closed the distance on the ATV. The rider glanced back over his shoulder. He spotted Frank and swerved left. Frank followed.

As Joe topped the rise, the ATV skidded. The four-wheeler was trapped between the brothers and a large pond. Joe barreled down the slope, switching on his headlight and angling straight for the ATV.

The headlight surprised the rider, and he swerved suddenly to the right. The ATV's tires skidded on the fog-slick grass, and it went into a spin.

Joe clamped down on his brakes, but they didn't catch. He slid toward the spinning four-wheeler, unable to stop. Frank, too, skidded headlong toward the impending pileup.

Both Hardys braced themselves for a spectacular three-way crash.

The Hardy Boys Mystery Stories

Available from MINSTREL Books and ALADDIN Paperbacks

THE **HARDY BOYS**®

#165
CRIME IN THE CARDS

FRANKLIN W. DIXON

Aladdin Paperbacks
New York London Toronto Sydney Singapore

This book is a work of fiction. Any references to historical events, real people, or real locales are used fictitiously. Other names, characters, places, and incidents are the product of the author's imagination, and any resemblance to actual events or locales or persons, living or dead, is entirely coincidental.

First Aladdin Paperbacks edition April 2002
First Minstrel edition January 2001

ALADDIN PAPERBACKS
An imprint of Simon & Schuster
Children's Publishing Division
1230 Avenue of the Americas
New York, NY 10020

Printed in the U.S.A.

10 9 8 7 6 5 4

THE HARDY BOYS and THE HARDY BOYS MYSTERY STORIES are trademarks of Simon & Schuster, Inc.

ISBN 0-7434-0659-1

Contents

CRIME IN THE CARDS

1 Creature Cards

"My White Knight jumps over your Spike Wall and attacks your Goblin Legion," Chet Morton said, a grin breaking out across his broad face. He laid down a card labeled "White Knight."

"Your hero may be smiling now," Tim Lester said, "but he doesn't know that behind my Spike Wall is a River of Snakes." He pulled the card from his hand and placed it faceup on the table.

"My knight laughs at your River of Snakes. They can't bite through his Enchanted Armor."

Tim frowned and scratched his head. "Then I guess I'll have to call in my War Giant for reinforcement."

The pretty blond girl seated at the other end of the lunchroom table frowned. "I don't get it," Callie Shaw said to the three friends seated with her.

"Me neither," Iola Morton agreed. Chet's sister

1

sighed and pulled her short brown hair into a pony-tail. "I figured this game was just another of Chet's passing fancies, but he's stuck with it a lot longer than he did with turtle racing."

Frank Hardy, a tall, athletic high school senior with dark hair and brown eyes, smiled. "The game's fairly simple," he said. "Each player is a Creature Commander and is trying to build up a deck of cards representing a vast fantasy army." Pretending an empty milk carton was a game-playing piece, he pushed it across the lunch table toward his seventeen-year-old brother, Joe Hardy. Joe responded by shoving an empty plastic cup out to "face" the carton.

"Then each commander pits his army against the other player's army," Joe said. "Whoever comes out on top is the King Creature Commander. It's not my type of game but . . ." He shrugged his wide shoulders, and his blue eyes twinkled.

"But you'll pretend you know all about it to impress the girls," Chet called from the other end of the table. He and Tim were still hunched over their colorful decks. Chet grinned at the Hardy brothers before returning to his game.

"You're awfully cocky for a guy who'd never heard of Creature Cards eight weeks ago, Chet," Iola called back.

Chet played one final card and lifted his arms with a victorious whoop. Tim rolled his eyes and leaned back in his seat. Chet scooped up his deck and scooted his chair down along the cafeteria floor to where his sister and the others were sitting.

"Hey," Chet said, laying his deck on the table, "I have a right to be smug. I just kicked Tim's Goblins all the way back to Valhalla."

Tim scooted his chair down to join the others as well. "You wouldn't have won if your Bargeist didn't pop up from your deck just now," he said.

"Bargeist?" Iola asked.

"I thought Valhalla was reserved for Viking heroes," Callie added.

"Anything goes in this game," Chet replied, thumping his wide chest. "And to the boldest commander goes victory."

"What Chet means," Frank said, "is that the game's creators aren't too concerned about mixing their mythologies."

"Who cares what they mix when they've created a card game this cool?" Tim interjected.

Chet nodded. "Besides, Troy King and his partners have made a fortune since they invented this game. They must know what they're doing; they're overnight millionaires. It's a lot more lucrative than the *detective* business." Chet grinned slyly at the Hardys.

"No wonder," Callie said, "the way you and your friends throw away money on those cards."

Frank put his hands behind his head and leaned back in his chair. "We may never be millionaires," he said, "but Joe and I have something more worthwhile."

"Callie and me?" Iola put in hopefully.

Joe smiled at his girlfriend. "Well, that, too," he said. "But I think Frank meant *character*."

"I hear *poverty* builds character," Chet countered.

"I've got plenty of characters," Tim added, laying his cards out on the table one by one. "I've got the Goblin Laird, the Samurai Scorpion, the Terrible Troll. . . . I've even got Sinbad and his Sister. Now, if only I had something to counter Chet's Bargeist! I need to come up with an anti-Chet strategy before the tournament next week."

"I didn't know they were holding a nerd convention this lunch period," a deep voice said. The Hardys and their friends turned to see Sam Kestenberg standing behind them. Sam was a tall, broad-shouldered senior with brown eyes and hair to match. "You kids still playing card games?" Sam asked disdainfully. "What's next, paper dolls?"

"Sam," Joe said coolly, "I almost didn't recognize you without your black leather jacket. You lose a bet or something?"

"Very funny, Hardy," Sam said. "You know that coats have to be stored in lockers during school hours."

Frank leaned forward in his chair, an expression of sympathy plastered on his face. "Aren't you afraid your rep will be ruined going out in public without it? People might think you're here to *learn*."

Kestenberg propped both his hands on the table; Chet scooped his cards out of the way. Kestenberg glowered at the Hardys.

"Listen, wise guys," he began, but just then the principal, Mr. Chambers, walked over to the group.

"Mr. Kestenberg," Mr. Chambers said, "I don't believe that you cleared away your lunch tray. You don't want to make extra work for the staff, do you?" His tone made it clear that Kestenberg should pick up his tray.

"Yeah, whatever," Kestenberg said grudgingly. He turned and walked over to a table with a lone tray sitting on it. The principal followed him.

"After you're done, Kestenberg," the principal said, "Mr. McCool wants to see you in print shop."

"Yeah, right," Kestenberg grumbled.

Iola turned to her friends and frowned. "I was glad when they kicked Sam Kestenberg off the football squad," she said.

"They didn't kick him off," Joe said. "He had to quit after he injured his knee."

"He got into enough trouble before then, though," Callie said. "Remember the time he rode his motorcycle around the track before the homecoming game? He nearly ran over the cheerleading squad."

"Kestenberg may be a jerk," Frank said, "but to give him credit, he was a pretty good ball player."

"Yeah," Joe said. "And I wouldn't wish a knee injury on anyone—even my worst enemy. Now, what was this about a Creature Cards tournament, Tim?"

"Next week, downtown in the Sullivan Hotel ballroom," Tim said.

"It's going to be great," Chet added. "Scores will

count toward national player rankings. Troy King himself is coming to hand out prizes."

"Naturally you're going," Frank said.

"Naturally," Chet replied. "The top winner gets a very rare card as part of the prize package. I hope you guys will come along to cheer me on."

"Sure," Joe said. "We love primeval card battles. Right, girls?"

"I can't wait," Iola said, rolling her eyes.

"I might have a meeting that night," Callie said. "Otherwise, I'll be happy to go." She smiled at Chet, who smiled back.

"If this is part of your strategy, Morton," Tim said jokingly, "then I'll have to secure my own cheering section."

Just then the bell rang.

Principal Chambers, who had gone back to patrolling the cafeteria, declared in a loud voice, "Pack your cards away, gentlemen and ladies. It's time to abandon your fantasy worlds for a return trip to the real one."

Chet and Tim pocketed their cards, as did several players sitting at other tables.

"You all want to go for a soda after class?" Frank asked.

Callie nodded. "Sounds great," she replied. "Let's meet by the gym."

"See you then," Joe said, waving to Iola and the others.

"I'll pass," Tim said. "I need to work on anti-Chet Creature Card strategies."

"I guess you'll be skipping school for the next week, then," Chet replied with a grin.

After school let out, Frank, Joe, Iola, and Callie met in front of the gym. As they were waiting for Chet, Tim Lester walked by.

"Hey, Tim," Joe said. "I thought you weren't coming."

"I'm not," Tim replied. "I was wondering if anyone knows what's up with Daphne Soesbee? I wanted to talk to her about the tournament, but she said she's too upset to talk."

"Does she play Creature Cards, too?" Frank asked.

"Yeah," said Tim. "She's one of the best players in school."

"I heard that someone broke into her locker," Iola said helpfully.

"Did anything get taken?" Joe asked.

"I think so," Iola said, "but I have no idea what."

Chet strolled up and joined his friends. "What's happening?" he asked.

"Daphne Soesbee got ripped off," Tim said.

"I just saw her talking to Gerry Wise and Peter Kaufmann," Chet said. "Or, should I say, I saw Gerry and Pete *trying* to talk to her. I thought she looked too wrung out to be discussing anything."

"Maybe we should get the whole story," Frank said. He led the others toward the student parking lot.

"I hope Daphne's cards weren't stolen," Chet said as they walked. "That would really set her back."

They quickly spotted Daphne. Her short-cropped

red hair and black leather jacket stood out in any crowd. As the Hardys and their friends drew closer, they saw her talking to Gerry Wise, a short junior with curly black hair and thick glasses.

Daphne wiped something, probably tears, from her cheeks. Then, before the Hardys could reach her, she climbed onto her small maroon motorcycle and took off. Gerry shrugged and started across the lot.

"Look at Daphne go," Joe said.

"Good thing the weather's been so warm for early winter," Iola said, "or she'd freeze to death riding that cycle."

"I guess we can find out what happened tomorrow," Frank said. "Daphne didn't look like she wanted to chat anyway."

"So, who's for something to eat?" Chet asked, grinning.

"I'll pass," Tim said. "I need to catch up with Gerry. Then I want to hit the Dungeon Guild to see about some new cards."

"You'll definitely need new cards to beat me on Tuesday," Chet said jovially. "You've only got six days to get your act together."

"That Bargeist isn't always going to save you," Tim replied. He walked to his old VW and waved goodbye to the others.

"The way you two carry on, you'd think the world revolved around Creature Cards," Iola said.

"Doesn't it?" Chet asked wryly.

* * *

The next morning was unseasonably warm. The Hardys, their girlfriends, and Chet hooked up before school in the cafeteria. The Bayport High breakfast program was in full swing, and students munched happily on bagels, cereal, pancakes, and bacon and eggs.

Scattered throughout the room, small groups of kids sat playing Creature Cards.

"I was on the phone with Tim last night," Chet said, speaking around a mouthful of bacon. "Turns out I was right."

Joe took a sip of orange juice and asked, "About what?"

"Daphne's Creature Cards got stolen," Chet said. "Somebody swiped them while she was in phys ed."

"You card players have a pretty good grapevine," Callie noted.

"They gossip like Aunt Gertrude does when she plays bridge," Joe said jokingly.

"Did Daphne tell anyone about the theft?" Frank asked.

"I don't know," Chet said. "Some other players have had cards ripped off, too, but I don't think anyone's gone to the police."

"They should," Frank said.

"The cops wouldn't take the complaint seriously," Chet replied. "They'd just think Creature Cards were a joke."

"Some of the cards are valuable, aren't they?" Joe asked.

"Yeah, some," Chet said, draining a carton of milk.

"My Bargeist is worth quite a bit. It's a very rare card, and powerful besides. I've seen Bargeists on the Net for over a hundred dollars."

"Yow!" said Iola. "No wonder you treat those cards like gold."

Chet nodded. "I picked up a good card last night, too. You want to see?" He stood up, fished into his pants pocket, and pulled out his deck.

"Maybe later," Frank said, checking his watch. "The bell should be ringing any second."

All five of them looked up at the class bell, expecting it to ring, but the P.A. system crackled to life instead.

"Good morning, students," Principal Chambers's voice said. "We'll begin our day in just a minute, but before we do, I have an announcement to make. Because of a rash of disruptions, including some thefts, in our classrooms and facilities, Creature Cards will be banned from Bayport High."

2 When Cards Are Outlawed, Only Outlaws Will Have Cards

"That's not fair!" Chet said, a sentiment echoed by others. A rumble of discontent began to build in the cafeteria.

Someone laughed loudly. Chet and the Hardys turned to see Sam Kestenberg leaning against the back wall, grinning.

"People, people, settle down," bellowed Mr. Mc-Cool, one of the teachers monitoring the room. He was a print-shop owner who taught printing at Bayport High three times a week. Tall and muscular with a shaved head, he looked more like a pro wrestler than a teacher. "The announcement's not finished

11

yet," he said. "Please remain in your seats. You, too, Mr. Kestenberg."

"Students caught playing with the cards during school hours will have their decks confiscated," the principal's voice continued. "Anyone carrying Creature Cards today should put them in their lockers."

"What a stupid idea!" sneered Pete Kaufmann, a sharp-featured blond kid sitting at the next table. "Daphne's cards got taken from her locker!"

As Pete spoke, many in the room glanced toward Daphne Soesbee, who was sitting alone at a table near the door. She rested her chin in her hands and looked miserable.

"Take the cards home tonight, and don't bring them back," Principal Chambers continued. "This decision will be strictly enforced. Photocopies of the new policy will be handed out to each student in homeroom. That is all."

The P.A. clicked off and the bell rang.

"I know many of you are unhappy about this decision," Mr. McCool said. "Sometimes, though, we have to roll with the punches. Let's all have a good day today."

The cafeteria doors opened, and everyone began to file out. The card players folded up their decks and put them away.

"I can't believe this," Chet said, pounding his fist on the table in frustration. "It's like we're outlaws all of a sudden."

"Poor Daphne is taking it hard," Callie said.

"She has some serious deck rebuilding to do if she wants to compete in that tournament," Chet noted.

"Chet, you dope," Iola said, "I think Callie means that Daphne could use some friends right now. She just transferred to Bayport this semester, after all."

"We should talk to her," Frank suggested. "Find out what she knows about her cards."

"Yeah," Joe said. "Maybe we can figure out who took them."

When they looked up, though, Daphne had already blended into the crowd of students leaving the lunchroom.

"We'll try to catch up with her later," Frank said.

"By then," Chet moaned, "we probably won't even be able to *talk* about the cards!"

Frank didn't catch up with Daphne until just after lunch, when he went to English with her. Chet and Tim were in that class, as well.

Daphne, however, didn't want to talk to Frank—or anyone else. She sat near the back of the room and sulked, her short red hair drooping over her hazel eyes.

As Mr. Pane bustled about, Chet leaned over to Tim. "When you get a minute," Chet said, "I've got something to show you. I picked it up at the Dungeon Guild last night."

"A card?" Tim said. "But we're not supposed to have them in class."

"I know," Chet replied, "but after what happened

to Daphne, I didn't want to put my deck in my locker. I'll show you when we get a minute."

"Better cool it, you two," Frank whispered from behind them.

Chet and Tim nodded and turned to face the front of the class.

Mr. Pane called the class into session a few moments later. He led a spirited discussion of the characters and symbolism in Herman Melville's *Moby Dick*.

"That white whale would make a great creature," Chet whispered across the aisle to Tim.

Tim nodded and whispered back. "What do you think, attack of nine and defense of four?"

"Nah," Chet said, shaking his head. "Defense would have to be more like six. A whale's easy to hit but hard to damage."

"And as a special power, it could swallow another character whole," Tim said gleefully.

"I'd be happy," Mr. Pane said, "if this special power didn't disrupt class. Lester, Morton, consider this a warning."

Tim and Chet nodded glumly.

Mr. Pane turned from the duo to Frank and said, "Frank, what do you think the sea gulls that circle Moby Dick symbolize?"

"Well . . ." Frank replied, "sea gulls live near shore, so they could represent a longing for home on the part of the sailors. On the other hand, they accompany Moby Dick, which suggests they're actually a false hope—the kind of desire that leads men to their doom."

The discussion continued until a message over the P.A. system called Mr. Pane from the room to take a phone call. "Study the final chapters while I'm gone," the teacher said. "When I return, we'll talk about Queequeg's coffin."

For a few minutes Chet studied his book. Then his enthusiasm got the better of him. He leaned over to Tim and said, "Tim, check this out."

From his pocket, Chet drew out a Creature Card.

"Wow!" Tim said, his eyes growing bright. "The Coyote! That's a demigod card I've never seen."

"I got it last night. It's not as rare as the Bargeist," Chet said, "and it doesn't have as good an attack number. But Coyote's better on defense. Plus, he's immune to most magic—only spells from the Supernatural Sphere can affect him."

"Way cool," Tim said. "But Sinbad and his Sister could still kick Coyote's tail. Is that a blood spatter on the corner of the card?"

"No, it's ketchup."

"Chet . . ." Frank's voice broke in.

"What is it, Frank?" Chet asked, slightly annoyed. "Can't you see we're—"

"Breaking the rules, Morton?" said Mr. Pane. He'd returned to the room a moment before, as Chet and Tim were busy talking.

"Mr. Pane," Chet said, "we were just—"

"I can see what you were 'just,' Morton. Now *just* hand the deck over to me."

Chet's face broke into a forlorn expression. Mr. Pane held out his palm, and Chet handed over the card he was holding.

"The others as well, please," Mr. Pane said.

Chet dug into his pocket and produced the rest of the deck.

Mr. Pane straightened the cards into a neat pile and walked with them to his desk. He opened the middle drawer and put the cards in. Then he drew a key out of his pocket and locked the drawer.

"You can reclaim the cards at the end of the school day," Mr. Pane said to Chet. "And, Morton . . ."

"Yes, sir?"

"Don't bring them to my class again, or you won't get them back."

Chet swallowed. "Yes, Mr. Pane."

Chet moved like a zombie through the rest of his classes, his mind on nothing but reclaiming his Creature Cards.

"I can't believe you were so . . . stupid," Iola said to her brother as she, Callie, and the Hardys gathered next to Chet's locker at the end of the day. "After the announcement and the photocopied rules and everything. What were you thinking?"

"My enthusiasm got the better of me," Chet said glumly. "That Coyote card was burning a hole in my pocket. I *had* to show it to someone."

"Too bad you didn't wait until after school," Callie said.

"Hey," Joe interjected, "I think Chet feels bad enough already."

Frank put an arm around Chet's shoulders. "Cheer up," he said. "You'll have those cards back before you can say 'King Creature Commander.' "

Just then Gerry Wise wandered by. "Hey Chet-man," Gerry said. "Bummer about your cards. Everybody's talking about it." Gerry pushed his black-framed glasses up on the bridge of his long nose and smiled sympathetically.

"Everybody?" Chet asked forlornly.

"Well, all of the Creature Card players," Gerry said. "Bad news travels fast. I saw some people trading cards before you got busted but after . . ." He formed his fingers into a goose egg. "Nada."

"Well, if people think this is going to slow me down," Chet said, "they're sadly mistaken. I still intend to vanquish all comers at the tournament."

Gerry turned and walked toward the front doors of the school. "We shall see, my man," he called back. "We shall see."

"Is he a player?" Callie asked.

"Nope," Chet said. "He does a lot of card trading and selling, though."

"Makes some good dough on it, too, from what I hear," Joe added.

"Creature Cards is a seller's market," Chet said.

"Some people will pay almost anything for a card that helps their game strategy."

"Well, let's go get your cards back," Frank suggested. "Otherwise, your strategy is going to be sitting on the sidelines during that tournament."

The five of them went to Mr. Pane's classroom. They found the teacher organizing a shelf of books near the windows.

Chet rapped lightly on the door. "Mr. Pane," he said politely.

Mr. Pane turned and smiled. "Morton," he said, "I thought you might show up." He walked toward his desk. "Sorry I had to do that, but rules are rules—and I could hardly break a new rule on the day it was implemented."

"I understand," Chet said sympathetically. "I shouldn't have had the cards out."

"I'm glad you understand," Mr. Pane said. He pulled the desk key out of his pocket. "I meant what I said, though. I don't want to see these cards in my class again."

Chet nodded as Mr. Pane opened the drawer. Mr. Pane frowned. Chet's jaw dropped.

"What is it?" Frank asked.

"The cards," Chet said. "They're gone!"

3 Cardnapped Creatures

"Did you take the cards out of the desk?" Frank asked Mr. Pane.

The teacher shook his head. "No," he said. "I haven't even opened the drawer since I confiscated them." He pulled the drawer all the way out and emptied the contents, but there was no sign of the cards. "I don't understand it," he said. "They couldn't have just vanished!"

"Does anyone else have access to your desk?" Joe asked.

"Normally, no," Mr. Pane said. "I had seventh period off today, though, and the room was empty. I was in the teachers' lounge. Anyone could have come in then, I guess. The desk was still locked, though."

Frank picked up the drawer and examined the lock.

"It doesn't look as though it's been forced," he said. "If it was picked, it was picked by an expert."

"I'll have to tell Principal Chambers," Mr. Pane said. "All of you wait here until I come back."

He went out the door and headed for the school offices.

Chet collapsed into a chair behind a student desk at the front of the room. He buried his face in his large hands. "I can't believe it," he said.

Iola walked over and put her hands on her brother's shoulders. "Don't worry, Chet," she said. "We'll find your cards."

"That deck had the Coyote *and* the Bargeist in it!" Chet moaned. "I have some spare cards at home, but how will I ever rebuild my deck in time for the tournament?"

"You could buy more," Callie suggested.

"At six dollars for a pack of thirteen?" Chet scoffed. "No way. Most of the cards in every pack are common cards—duplicates of ones I already have. It's taken me almost two months to build up that deck to tournament level through buying and trading. I don't have the time or money to replace the rare cards I've lost." He closed his eyes and rubbed his short blond hair distractedly.

"We'll just have to get your cards back, then," Joe said. He and Frank had been poking around the room, looking for any clues.

"Do you think you *can* find them?" Chet asked hopefully.

"We've solved tougher cases," Frank said. He replaced a row of books he'd been paging through. "I'm not finding anything here, though. How about you, Joe?"

Joe, who had been searching under the desk, stood up. "Nothing," he said. "Too many people use this room on a regular basis. We'd have to be pretty lucky to find a clue pointing directly to the culprit. Unless, of course, the robber got careless."

"Whoever opened that drawer knew what he was doing," Frank said. "A pro couldn't have done better."

Just then Mr. Pane returned with the principal. Chet stood up hopefully as they entered.

"I can't say that I'm really surprised about this," Mr. Chambers said.

"Well, *I'm* surprised," Mr. Pane replied. "No one's ever broken into my desk before."

"Those cards have been causing a lot of trouble in this school. It was your deck, Mr. Morton?" the principal asked.

Chet nodded.

"Were the cards valuable?"

"Some of them. Yeah." Chet said.

"I don't mean to sound unsympathetic," Principal Chambers said, "but this is one of the reasons I banned Creature Cards from school this morning. If you'd kept the cards in your locker, as I suggested, this wouldn't have happened. We'll look into it, of course, but we have a lot of students and we can't just interrogate everyone. We could call the police, though."

Chet shook his head. "No," he said. "The cops wouldn't take this seriously."

"Chet," Callie said, "alerting the police might be a good idea."

"I'd rather trust Joe and Frank," Chet said. "They'll get my cards back."

"Thanks, Chet," Frank said. "We'll try to live up to your faith in us."

"I'll talk to the other members of the faculty," Mr. Pane said hopefully. "With a little luck maybe we can turn them up."

"Thanks," Chet said. He and the others filed silently out of the classroom. They visited their lockers and then headed out to the student parking lot.

"Man," Joe said, "I hate locked-room mysteries. A locked desk is almost as bad."

"As you said, Joe, there are just too many people with access to that room," Frank noted.

"Well, whoever took Chet's cards had to know they were in that desk," Callie said. "Shouldn't that limit the suspects to the people who were in Mr. Pane's class at the time?"

"That might be true," Frank said, "if it weren't for the network of Creature Card players in the school. Remember what Gerry Wise said? The news about the cards being confiscated was all over school."

Callie frowned. "Oh, that's right," she said. "All the card players' being so close will sure make this tougher to solve. What about the lock, though? Who'd have the skill to pick it? Could you narrow the list of suspects that way?"

"It didn't look like a very tricky lock," Frank said. "Either Joe or I could have sprung it without leaving a mark."

"Plus," Joe said, "it's a standard issue school desk. There may be any number of keys for it floating around."

The group reached Frank and Joe's van.

"Let's go get pizza," Frank said. "We can discuss the case on the way."

"What about our cars?" Callie asked.

"We'll come back and pick them up later," Joe replied.

"Sounds good," said Iola.

All five of them piled into the Hardys' van and headed for the pizza shop.

"So, you think there could be another key to the desk?" Iola asked after they were under way.

Frank nodded. "It's possible. Any number of people could have a duplicate. Mr. Chambers probably does, for one."

Chet sighed. "But we *know* Chambers wouldn't swipe my cards. So where do we go from here? I'm sunk without that deck."

"We should talk to other players," Joe said. "Figure out who had a motive for taking your deck."

"That could be just about anyone," Chet said with a laugh. "Those cards are valuable. Whoever took them might just sell them. Some kids collect Creature

Cards without playing the game. They keep them as an 'investment.' Gerry's like that. He's got plenty of cards, but I've never seen him play. Daphne and I aren't the only ones who've had cards stolen, either. Just about everyone I know has had a card or two lost or stolen. We're the only ones who've had whole decks taken, though. And just a few days before the tournament." He shook his fist in anger. "I wish there was something I could do."

"Don't worry, Chet," Iola said. "I know it looks bad, but Frank and Joe will find them. You should concentrate on getting ready for the tournament. Maybe you could buy the cards you need from Gerry. You've gotten cards from him before, haven't you?"

"Yeah," Chet said. "But he bases his prices on the cost guides posted on the Internet—so shopping with Gerry is no bargain."

"I didn't realize there was so much money in this," Callie said.

Chet nodded. "A lot of kids sink their savings into their decks. I know people who spend most of the money they earn at their part-time jobs on the game. I've done it myself—once or twice."

"Do you think all the thefts are tied together?" Iola asked Joe.

"Maybe not all, but it seems likely that some are," Joe replied. "What burns me up is that kids are getting hit at both ends. They pay dealers a lot for the cards initially, and then they have to replace their stolen cards."

"It's just a big circle of cash," Frank agreed. He

pulled the van up in front of the pizza shop. Inside they sat at a booth and ordered two pizzas and a pitcher of root beer.

"Chet," Joe asked, "how good do you think your chances really were in the tournament?"

"Pretty good," Chet said glumly.

"Who are your main competitors?" Frank asked.

"Well, the tournament will draw people from all over the state, and not just kids, either. The game is big business, and people take tournaments very seriously. So, it's hard to predict who might show up. Locally, though, the toughest players are Pete Kaufmann and Daphne Soesbee."

"And Daphne's missing her cards, too," Callie said. "That puts Pete in a pretty good position."

"I guess it does," Chet said. "I never thought of that."

"What about Tim?" Iola asked. "You play against him all the time."

"Yeah," Chet said. "That's why I'm not really worried about him. I know his moves pretty well."

"Speaking of Tim . . ." Frank said, looking through the big storefront window. "Isn't that him walking up the street?"

All of them looked. Sure enough, Tim Lester came strolling down the sidewalk past the pizzeria. He spotted the group sitting inside, waved, and entered the restaurant.

"Hey, guys," Tim said, a broad smile lighting up his face. "Chet, wait till you see what I got." He sat down at the table and fished his deck out of his jacket pocket.

He laid the cards out on the table, fanned through them, and plucked out one showing a picture of a large monster that looked like a giant robot. "Check this," Tim said. "Titanium Titan, very rare, very powerful. Might even give me the edge I need against your Bargeist, Chet."

The Hardys and the girls glanced uncomfortably at one another, realizing that Tim didn't know about Chet's cards. Chet's eyes, though, remained fixed on Tim's deck, fanned out on the table.

Suddenly Chet's hand flashed out and grabbed one of the cards from the deck. He held it up just inches from Tim's face. Frank and Joe saw that it was a Coyote card—one of the ones Chet had lost.

"Where did you get this?" Chet angrily asked Tim. "Did you steal it from me?"

4 Dungeon Guild

"What are you talking about?" Tim asked, flustered.

"Someone stole Chet's cards out of Mr. Pane's desk," Joe said.

"You mean you didn't get your cards back?" Tim asked Chet.

Chet wasn't listening, though. His face was still red with anger. "Where did you get this Coyote?" he asked. "They're very rare. Mine was the only one in Bayport."

"Well, not anymore," Tim said, getting angry himself. "I picked that up at the Dungeon Guild just forty-five minutes ago. Do you want to see my receipt?"

"If you don't mind," Frank said.

Scowling, Tim fished into his pocket again.

"Wait a minute," Chet said, the color of his round face returning to normal. "This isn't my card. It doesn't have that ketchup stain in the corner. Oh, man! I'm sorry, Tim. I'm just so upset about my deck."

"How did your cards get stolen?" Tim asked.

"Someone picked the lock on Mr. Pane's desk and took them," Callie offered.

"Hold on a second," Joe said. "What's this about a ketchup stain?"

"Well . . ." Chet said sheepishly, "I was so excited when I got the Coyote in a card pack, that I got kind of careless. I was eating a burger while I rearranged my deck to fit the Coyote in. Some ketchup dripped out of the bun and on to the cards. I blotted it off, but you could still see a red stain."

"I remember," Tim said. "When you showed me the Coyote I thought the stain was blood."

"Yeah, the same drop of ketchup spilled on the corner of one of my White Knights, too." Chet shrugged sheepishly. "It's not as though the stain affects game play—it just makes the card worth less if I wanted to sell it."

"You gotta be more careful with your cards once you get them back," Tim said. "You've got a lot of dough tied up in that deck."

"I'm not in this for the money," Chet said. "I'm in it for the *fame.*" Then his face saddened again. "Right now, though, I'm not in it at all."

"So, there's no chance this card is one of yours, then?" Joe asked.

"No, I'm sure it's not mine," Chet answered. "Sorry I lost it with you, Tim."

Tim nodded. "That's okay, Chet. I understand. I'd be on edge, too, if I lost my deck. If there's anything I can do . . ."

"You said you got the Coyote at the Dungeon Guild," Frank said to Tim. "Did you buy it singly, or pick it up in a pack?"

"I bought it as a single," Tim said. "The odds of another pack with a Coyote showing up are pretty slim. There aren't that many Coyotes in the whole country, and the packs are distributed randomly. For two to show up in Bayport . . . Well, I'm sure the odds are against it."

"If they're so rare, how'd the Dungeon Guild happen to have a single one to sell you?" Frank asked.

Tim shrugged. "You'd have to ask Ron Felix—he owns the shop. Probably he got it through his network, though."

"People all over the country trade and sell cards," Chet explained. "A lot of them use the Internet, but there's plenty of trading by phone and in person, too."

"You'd be surprised how far a card can travel if the right money is involved," Tim said, smiling. "Before the crackdown, a lot of trading happened in school, too."

Just then Pete Kaufmann walked into the pizzeria. He started for the pick-up window but changed direction when he spotted Chet.

"Hey, Morton," he said as he walked up to the table. "I heard that your deck got ripped off."

Joe's eyes narrowed. "How'd you know about the

theft?" the younger Hardy asked. "We came here right after it happened."

"I was in the gym for fencing practice when Mr. Pane came in and talked to Coach Fazzio about it. Pane wanted all the teachers to keep an eye out for your deck." Pete smiled smugly and turned to Chet. "I guess that puts you out of the tournament, Morton. Too bad. Not that you stood a chance against me."

Chet stood defiantly. "Hey, I'm not out of it yet," he said. "I've got enough cards at home to enter, and there's plenty of time between now and then to re- place what I need."

"We're going to help him, too," Iola added defen- sively.

"Ooh! I'm scared," Pete said sarcastically. He turned and headed for the pick-up window.

"Remember, Kaufmann," Chet called after Pete, "it's the *player* who wins the games—not the cards."

"Hard to win a game without any cards," Pete shot back. He didn't even glance over his shoulder as he said it.

Chet glared at Pete's back as Pete picked up his order and walked out the door.

When the pizzas arrived everyone dug in, eating quietly for a while. Finally Chet broke the silence. "Man, Pete really bugs me sometimes."

"That's probably part of his strategy, big brother," Iola said. "Pete's one of those guys who likes to win at any cost. I've seen him fence. He's ruthless."

"You got that right, Iola" Tim said. "Pete boasts that

he's got over two thousand dollars tied up in his decks."

"He has more than one deck?" Joe asked.

"Lots of people do," Tim replied. "Before a tournament, they size up the competition, and then choose their card mix. I've got a couple of decks myself."

"I haven't been at it long enough to have more than one good deck," Chet said. "That's why I keep my spare cards—to make an extra deck when I can."

"That makes sense," Joe said. "The same way you might change the tune-up of your car for different types of races."

"What about Daphne," Frank asked. "Do you know if she has another deck?"

"She might," Chet replied. "Though I've only seen her use the one."

"So, Chet," Tim said, "if you've got a bunch of basic cards, maybe you can pick up some of the rest you need at the Dungeon Guild. Ron got a fresh supply of cards in today."

"That's a good idea," Frank said. "I'd like to talk to the owner—make sure he knows that Chet's cards have been stolen."

"With his connections, maybe he could get a line on Chet's deck," Joe added.

"I have to inventory my cards at home before I go," Chet said, "to figure out what I need."

"I'd be glad to help with that," Tim offered.

"Ha! I bet you would," Chet shot back playfully.

"That way you'd know exactly what cards you needed to beat me."

"Well, if you don't want my help . . ." Tim said in a hurt tone.

Seeing that Tim had taken him too seriously, Chet said, "I'm only kidding, Tim. But, if you want to help, we could have some tune-up games—after I start rebuilding. Maybe tomorrow, even. Tonight, Iola can help me inventory my cards."

"My brother doesn't think I have anything better to do than to help him count cards," Iola said, rolling her eyes. Joe smiled at his girlfriend and gave her hand a supportive squeeze.

"Well, I know that the rest of you are super-brains who never have to study," Callie said, "but I've got AP biology homework. I really should go home. You guys can call me later if you need help, though."

"I'd still like to talk to the Dungeon Guild owner tonight," Frank said. "Tomorrow at school we can speak with Gerry Wise about the theft."

"He probably already knows," Chet said glumly.

"That doesn't mean he couldn't help us out," Frank said. "If he sells cards regularly, maybe he'll hear something. We'll talk to some of the other players, too."

Joe stood. "Okay," he said. "We'll drop the three of you at the school parking lot to pick up your cars. Then Frank and I will go talk to the shop owner."

"Sounds good," Chet said, boxing up the leftover pizza.

"Can we drop you anywhere, Tim?" Frank asked as they were leaving.

"Nah," Tim said. "I parked my bike up the street. With the weather being so warm, I can use the exercise."

"Good idea," Joe said. "It won't stay warm much longer."

Tim said goodbye, and the Hardys drove the others back to their cars. On the way, Chet made up a list of his most valuable missing cards so that the Hardys could alert the owner of the Dungeon Guild to look for them.

It was almost dark by the time Frank and Joe parked their van a block away from the Dungeon Guild. The store was in a medium-size, single-story brick building in an older section of downtown Bayport. The painted sign over the entrance featured an armor-clad warrior and a fire-breathing dragon. Below the sign, two large picture windows displayed Creature Cards and many other games. A small sign hanging on the glass door proclaimed the Dungeon Guild's hours in Old English lettering.

The Hardys walked inside. The store was deserted except for a short, chubby, middle-aged man with a goatee and thinning black hair. The man was bustling around the store, arranging displays and setting up new merchandise. He looked up from a glass case when the Hardys entered.

"Hi. Welcome to the Dungeon Guild," he said. "Can I help you?"

"I'm Frank Hardy, and this is my brother, Joe. We're looking for the store owner," Frank said.

"That's me," the man said, hooking his thumb at his chest. "Ron Felix, proprietor. How can I help you guys?"

"We're friends of Chet Morton's," Joe said. "He got some Creature Cards stolen today and we wanted you to be on the lookout for them."

"Stolen cards—that's bad," Mr. Felix said. He wiped the sweat from his shiny brow with a handkerchief. "Do you have a list of the missing cards?"

"Yeah, right here," Joe said, handing over the list Chet had made up.

"Hmm. Tough luck for Chet," Mr. Felix said. "He's a good customer. There are a lot of prime cards on this list. Do you mind if I make a copy?"

"Please do," Frank said.

Mr. Felix walked over to a fax machine beside his cash register and ran the list through. A grainy copy came out the other side. Felix handed the original back to Joe. As he took the paper, Joe noticed a slight trembling in the store owner's hand.

"I'll keep an eye out for them," Felix said, flashing a quick smile at the brothers. "Don't get your hopes up, though. I don't deal in stolen cards."

"We never said you did," Frank said. "Just stay alert for them. We have a few other questions, too. Where do you get your stock? Tim Lester picked up a rare Coyote card here today, and that's one of the cards on Chet's list. Tim's Coyote wasn't the stolen one, but I'd like to know where you got the card."

"The main place I get cards is from my distributor," Felix said. "The same place I get all my new games. I get boxes of Creature Cards all the time. I got a new shipment yesterday." He wiped the sweat off his brow again.

"We heard you got some new cards today, too," Joe said. "Where'd they come from?"

"I buy cards from collectors nearly every day," Felix said.

"From people in town?" Frank asked.

"Sometimes," Felix replied, "but I get a lot more over the Internet—auction and trading sites and so forth. If I know a customer is looking for a card, I can usually turn one up within a week—unless it's really rare. I've got good connections." He smiled proudly and checked his watch.

"What about the single cards you sell, where do those come from?" Joe asked.

"Same places," Felix said. "A lot of them I get from collectors and traders. Other times, I'll open up a new carton or two to replenish my stocks. That's a little dicey, though, because you never know what you're going to get. Usually, I can count on getting a couple of rare cards in every box. The profit on those makes up for my selling the common cards cheap."

"Sounds kind of risky," Frank noted.

"Well, I wouldn't want to do it as an investment, the way some of these kids do," Felix said. "You're practically begging to be ripped off. Prices on cards change quickly and you never know when the market might crash. Remember when Bombo Bear trading cards were big?"

Joe and Frank nodded.

"Now . . . *nothing*. The Bombo cards are worthless. I can't give them away," Felix said. "The only thing they're good for is starting fires. I'm just glad I didn't have a lot of money tied up in Bombo inventory. I could sell you three boxes for ten dollars."

"No thanks," Frank said. "Do you think the bottom might fall out of the Creature Cards market?" he asked.

"Not any time soon," Felix replied. "Selling those cards is like a license to print money for Troy King and the other creators. And the game community is still strongly behind it. I wouldn't worry for another couple of years at least, but cards in a shoebox are no substitute for money in a bank account."

"What about that Coyote you sold Tim?" Frank asked. "Where did that come from?"

"A private collector sold it to me," Felix said. "I really shouldn't say any more. A lot of my customers want confidentiality. Game strategy, and all that."

He walked behind the register and bent down to straighten a number of card boxes in a glass case. Frank and Joe checked out the displays. Some of the cards were mounted in Lucite containers, like tiny pieces of art. A hefty price tag adorned each frame.

"So, can I get you guys anything?" Felix asked hopefully.

"Not today," Joe said. "We just came in to tell you about Chet's cards."

"Maybe some other time," Frank added.

"Okay. See ya," Felix said. He smiled once more and then returned to straightening his displays.

Frank and Joe left the store. Night had fallen while they were inside, and a light fog was creeping through the city. As they buttoned their coats, Joe said to Frank, "Not much to go on there."

Frank nodded. "Yeah. Did Mr. Felix seem nervous to you?"

"A bit," Joe said. "But maybe he's used to dealing with players instead of 'regular people.'" He smiled and his blue eyes twinkled.

"Come on," Frank said. "Let's head back home and call Chet to see how he's making out."

He and Joe started up the street to the car. As they did, Joe glanced back toward the store.

"That's funny," Joe said.

"What?" Frank asked.

"Mr. Felix just flipped the sign in the front window to Closed. But the schedule listed on the door said he'd be open another two hours," the younger Hardy replied.

"Perhaps something came up and he had to leave suddenly," Frank suggested.

Joe nodded. "Maybe. Or maybe something we said spooked him. Let's sit in the van for a while to see if anything happens."

He and Frank got into the van and watched the building. A streetlight gave them a good view of the door to the shop. A few minutes later Mr. Felix came out lugging two big boxes marked Cards. He looked

37

around as if checking to make sure no one was watching, then he crossed the street and got into a beat-up sedan.

Felix stuck his head out the driver's side window and checked the street one last time before starting the car. The sedan's old engine roared to life and Felix drove off into the fog—with his headlights *turned off*.

5 Rendezvous in the Dark

"A tad suspicious, don't you think?" Joe asked.

"Yeah," Frank said. "Let's tail him to see what he's up to." He started the van and followed Felix's car into the fog. Frank didn't turn on his headlights either.

"He was being pretty cautious," Joe said. "You'd better hang back a ways."

"As far as I can without losing him," Frank replied, his brown eyes peering intently through the mist. Fortunately, the streets were deserted and fairly well lit. Driving without lights wasn't too hazardous.

Three blocks later Felix turned a corner and switched on his lights.

The lights made the car easier to see, so Frank could hang back a bit more. When he'd given Felix enough space, Frank switched on his lights as well.

"Mr. Felix doesn't seem to be in a hurry," Joe said. "Maybe he just forgot to turn his lights on."

"Could be," Frank replied.

Felix's car turned one corner, then another, then a third.

"Hey," Joe said, "he's doubled back on himself."

"Either he doesn't know where he's going, or he's trying to make sure he isn't followed."

Joe nodded. "Why don't you cut over a block and get ahead of him."

"Good idea," Frank said. "It's harder tailing someone from in front, but not nearly as easy to get spotted."

The next time Felix turned, Frank turned as well. He swung down an alley and then across a school parking lot. When Frank hit the main road again, Joe spotted Felix's car out the rear window.

"Good work, Frank," Joe said.

"Help me keep an eye on him, Joe. Having another set of eyes is easier than using the mirrors all the time."

"Check," Joe replied. He left the passenger seat and sat, facing backward, on the seat behind his older brother.

With Joe's help, Frank kept the Hardys' van in front of the card dealer's car without arousing suspicion. Felix doubled back several more times, but—using his knowledge of the city—Frank stayed with him.

Finally, though, Felix turned down a street where Frank couldn't cut ahead of him.

"Don't worry," Joe said from the backseat. "That

street heads through the woods near Waterfront Park. There aren't any turn-offs for a while. If you double back quickly, we can get behind him again."

"Right," Frank said. He pulled a U turn and traced back to where Felix had turned. "Do you see him?" he asked as they pulled on to the road through the woods.

"Not yet," Joe said, taking the front passenger seat once more and buckling in.

"I'd hate to lose Felix after all this," Frank said.

Joe nodded. He scanned the darkened scenery outside. Skeletal trees with only a few brown leaves clinging to their branches flashed by the windows. Joe saw footpaths, but nothing large enough for a car to take.

Frank kept his eyes fixed on the road ahead, seeking the sedan's taillights. After a few more minutes he accepted defeat. "I'm afraid we've lost him."

Joe was about to agree with Frank, when he spotted something. "That deserted parking lot on the left," he said. "I think I saw a sedan sitting in there."

"I'll pull over up ahead," Frank said. "Get the binoculars out and we'll check."

Joe went to the rear of the van and dug out the binoculars and two flashlights after Frank pulled over. They locked up the van and sprinted back to the parking lot entrance. A short driveway through the trees led to a large paved area adjoining a playground.

"That's Felix's car, all right," Joe said, squinting into the darkness.

"Keep to the trees," Frank whispered. "We don't want him seeing us."

Joe nodded and the two of them cut into the woods by the side of the road. When they reached the edge of the playground they spotted two figures standing by a swing set on the far side of the clearing.

Joe put the binoculars to his eyes. "That's Felix," he said. "But I can't tell who's with him—the person is wearing a hat and a heavy coat."

"Let's get closer," Frank whispered.

The two of them skirted the woods, trying to remain hidden. It was tricky maneuvering through the undergrowth in the foggy darkness, but the Hardys managed it without making much noise.

Drawing closer, the Hardys saw the two card boxes on a picnic table between the figures. Felix handed some cards to the other person; the person in the hat then gave Felix money. The Hardys couldn't make out any more details through the darkness.

Just then the card dealer tucked his boxes under his arm and headed back toward his sedan. Felix's customer jogged toward the woods on the far side of the swing set.

"You follow Felix," Joe whispered. "I'll tail the other one."

"Check," Frank said. He cut through the woods, angling himself for the card dealer's car. Joe ran quietly in the opposite direction.

Frank reached the sedan at about the same time

Felix did. He walked up just as the card dealer was opening the door.

"Mr. Felix . . ." Frank said.

Felix nearly jumped out of his skin.

"It's Frank Hardy," Frank said. "I was wondering what you're doing out here."

"I—I could ask you the same thing," Felix stammered. He mopped his forehead with a handkerchief he retrieved from his pocket. "Were you following me?" he asked angrily.

"Why did you close up shop just after we left?" Frank asked. "Your sign said you were supposed to be open for another two hours."

"I had some business to conduct," Felix replied.

"In a park, at night?" Frank said skeptically.

"Look," Felix said stiffly, "I don't owe you any explanation."

"Well, with so many Creature Cards being stolen lately," Frank said, "maybe you'd rather explain all this to the police."

Felix rubbed his head. "I'm sorry if I've been rude," he said, quickly back-pedaling. "But you frightened me. I thought I was alone here—aside from my client."

"So you came here to sell cards?" Frank said. "Why?"

"This close to a tournament, some players don't want to be seen in the shop," Felix said. "They're afraid that competitors will find out what they've bought. Knowledge of a player's deck can tip the balance in a Creature Cards game. For some of my better customers, I'll make a personal delivery if the cards are valuable enough."

"So, who's this client?"

Mr. Felix's face grew stern. "I won't tell you that," he said. "This client is paying for confidentiality. You can take me to the police station if you want, but I won't answer that question. It would hurt my business if I broke faith."

"Why didn't you go to the client's house?" Frank asked.

"My client didn't want to chance it," Felix said. "This park is remote enough that no one should have found us." He frowned at Frank, as if disappointed that his careful scheme had failed. "Well," he continued, "I have other things to do. So, unless you're taking me to the police station, I'm going to leave."

"I'll keep the police informed," Frank said, "but you don't need to see them right this minute."

Felix placed the card boxes on the passenger seat and slipped in beside them. Frank watched Felix's taillights disappear into the fog. Then he walked back across the park to where he'd last seen Joe.

A few minutes later the younger Hardy came jogging out of the woods on the far side of the playground.

"Did you catch him?" Frank asked.

Joe shook his head while he caught his breath. "No such luck," he said. "There's another parking lot on the far side of the trees. By the time I got there, I didn't see anyone. I did hear an engine driving away, though. It sounded like an ATV or a motorcycle."

Frank rubbed his chin. "Hmm. A lot of people use ATVs and dirt bikes in this park during good weather," he said. "With this warm snap, the sound you heard might not have anything to do with the case."

Joe shrugged. "Hard to tell. I'm wiped out. Let's call it a day."

Frank nodded and the two returned to their van. On the way home, Frank filled Joe in on what Felix had told him.

The next morning the weather was still unseasonably warm. When the Hardys pulled into the student lot at school, they saw several groups of kids sitting on the hoods of their cars, playing Creature Cards.

Daphne stood in one corner of the lot talking to Pete Kaufmann. She looked a bit forlorn; Pete a bit smug. The two chatted animatedly. Tim Lester approached them but turned away at some jibe from Pete that the Hardys couldn't hear. Tim joined another group of players nearby.

Gerry Wise roamed between the gaming groups, watching, and occasionally selling cards to some of the younger players.

The Hardys spotted Chet, Iola, and Callie hanging out on the far side of the lot.

"How'd you make out?" Callie called to the brothers as they approached. She smiled and the morning sun made her blond hair sparkle like gold. Frank gave her a quick hug.

"Learned a little; wasted a lot of time," Joe replied.

"Mr. Felix made a late delivery to one of his customers," Frank said, "but he wouldn't tell us who that customer was."

Chet nodded. "I've heard that he makes deliveries, but I've never spent enough money to earn the service myself."

"How'd it go with you?" Joe asked Iola.

Joe's girlfriend rolled her eyes. "I spent a thrilling evening cataloging all things hideous with my brother," she said. She smiled to show that she didn't really mind the job.

"At least I know what cards I need now," Chet said. "I came up with a good idea to help find my stolen deck, too."

Sam Kestenberg's voice drifted in from nearby, "What's your plan, Morton?" he asked as he walked over to the group. "You gonna cry until someone gives you your cards back?" Kestenberg laughed and adjusted the collar of his leather jacket.

Chet balled his hands into fists, but Joe stepped in front of his friend.

"I don't recall inviting you to join our conversation, Kestenberg," the younger Hardy said.

Kestenberg sneered. "I don't recall needing your permission, Hardy. You guys need to get *real* lives. All this card stuff is making you soft."

"Keep it up and you'll find out how soft we are," Joe said.

"Did you want something, Kestenberg," Frank asked, "or are you just spending your morning bothering people?"

"It's a free country," Kestenberg replied.

"Come on," Joe suggested. "Let's go inside. All of a sudden, the air out here stinks." He turned and walked toward the school. Chet, Iola, and the others followed.

As they passed Kestenberg, the ex-football player stuck out his foot.

Joe tripped and landed heavily against a nearby car. The car's alarm went on, and one of the card players came running from the other side of the lot to turn it off.

Joe spun on Kestenberg. "That's all I'm going to take from you," the younger Hardy growled.

Kestenberg waved Joe forward with a hand and smiled. "Bring it on, Blondie," he said.

6 Bayport's Most Wanted

A crowd quickly gathered around Sam Kestenberg and Joe; everyone stopped playing Creature Cards and came to watch.

Frank seemed about to step in, but Joe warned him back. "Keep out of this, Frank," he said. "This is between Kestenberg and me."

"Good," Kestenberg said. "I've been aching to get a piece of you since I quit the football team. I couldn't punch you out then because we were teammates, but now . . ."

"Frank, do something!" Iola cried.

"Kestenberg has it coming," Frank said coolly. "Don't worry. Joe can take care of himself."

"I don't like Joe fighting my fights," Chet grumbled.

"Just keep out of it," Callie said. "I don't think this was about you, anyway."

Joe stepped forward, ready for action.

"Stop right there!" a loud voice called.

Everyone in the lot turned to see Mr. McCool, the printing teacher, walking toward them from the faculty parking lot. His mouth was set in a thin line, and his brows were knitted together just below his shaved head. He looked like a pro wrestler heading for the ring.

Kestenberg straightened up and Joe stepped away from him. The rest of the crowd started to disperse, but McCool said, "Freeze. Every one of you. Nobody leaves until I'm done here."

"We were just—" Kestenberg began.

"I know what you were doing," Mr. McCool said. "And you're lucky I don't drag both of you to Mr. Chambers's office. Be glad that I just work here part-time. I'm not on the clock, yet, so I've got a little flexibility in dealing with this situation."

McCool scanned the group, resting his steel gray eyes on each student in turn. "These are school grounds," McCool said, "for those of you who need to be reminded. Among other things, that means there will be no brawling in this lot. *And,*" he continued, "Creature Cards are banned *here* as well as in the school building itself."

A collective gasp went up from the gathered kids. Gerry Wise went pale, and Daphne Soesbee edged toward the back of the crowd. Pete Kaufmann folded his arms across his chest. Sweat beaded on Tim Lester's forehead.

"I could confiscate every card in this lot," McCool said, his voice as cold as ice.

"Mr. McCool," Tim said, his voice almost squeaking, "we didn't mean to do anything wrong."

"I figured that," McCool said, "which is why I'm cutting you all a break." He folded his arms across his brawny chest. "I'm going to go into the building to punch in. When I come out again, I don't want to see any sign of those cards on school grounds. You understand?"

The gathered students nodded their heads. Kestenberg snickered.

"Kestenberg," McCool said, fixing his steely gaze on the ex-football player, "you come with me."

"That's not fair!" Kestenberg said.

"You think it would be more fair if I took you to the principal's office?" McCool asked. "Move it!" The teacher turned and left; Kestenberg reluctantly trailed after him.

"Boy," Chet said quietly, "Mr. McCool should have been a gym teacher."

"Well, I don't see any reason to hang out here," Callie said. "Let's go inside."

"Just a second," Frank interrupted. "I want to ask Gerry Wise a few questions before we go in."

Frank scanned the lot. The card players were standing around, staring suspiciously at one another. Some tucked their cards into their backpacks, others put them in their cars. A few just stuffed decks into their pockets. Clearly, no one wanted anyone else to know where his cards were hidden. Frank saw no sign of Gerry, though.

"Boy, he sure vanished fast," Chet said.

"Probably he had the most cards to lose," Frank noted. "I don't see Daphne, Tim, or Pete hanging around, either."

"Don't worry about it, Frank," Joe said. "We'll catch up to them later." The five friends walked toward the front entrance.

"Hey, Chet, I almost forgot . . ." Callie said. "What was your plan for getting your cards back?"

"Iola and I made some Wanted posters last night," Chet said. "I'm offering a cash reward for anyone who turns in my deck—no questions asked."

"How much?" Joe asked.

"One hundred and fifty dollars," Chet said. "They're worth more than that, but I'm hoping that whoever took them would rather have the money than the hassle of trying to fence them."

Frank frowned. "I don't know, Chet," he said. "Sometimes rewards scare up a lot of false information."

"I'm not offering anything for information," Chet said, "unless it leads *directly* to the return of the cards. And I didn't put the amount on the poster, just some contact info. I figured if I put too much on the posters, Mr. Chambers might not let me them put up."

"Well, it's a start anyway," Joe said.

"I guess it really couldn't do any harm," Frank added.

"If nothing else, maybe the posters will shake something loose for you guys to work on," Chet said.

"There's only one way to find out," Frank replied.

Chet went to the principal's office to obtain permission to put up his posters. The Hardys, Iola, and Callie volunteered to help Chet put the flyers up.

Even with Creature Cards banned, Bayport High was buzzing about the upcoming tournament. Frank and Joe chatted with some of the other players, and surreptitiously listened in on as many conversations as they could, but they didn't find out anything new.

Sam Kestenberg hassled the brothers whenever he saw them. The Hardys ignored Kestenberg's comments about their hanging with "nerds" and "losers." Eventually, Kestenberg found other people to bother.

During lunch, the Hardys and their girlfriends met with Chet. He had permission to hang the posters at lunchtime, and seemed pleased with himself. In fact, he looked happier than he had since his cards were stolen.

"I talked to Mr. Pane today and I think he feels guilty," Chet said when the five of them were outside the cafeteria.

"You can't blame him for the theft," Callie said. "How could he know someone would break into his desk?"

"I *don't* blame him," Chet countered. "But if he wants to feel guilty . . . well, maybe I can use that later when I'm late with an assignment." He smiled.

"We should split up," Frank said. "Lunch period isn't going to last forever."

The others nodded their agreement, but before they could split up, Pete wandered by on his way to the cafeteria.

"Getting desperate, Morton?" he asked.

"There's plenty of time before the tournament next week," Chet said defensively. "I'm just trying to cover all my bases."

"I guess that means you're not having much luck rebuilding your deck," Pete said.

"He's hardly started!" Iola blurted out.

Pete smiled smugly. "If I were you, Morton, I'd have rebuilt by now. There's more than one way to get cards for a tournament." He winked slyly and walked into the cafeteria.

Daphne Soesbee, who had been waiting in line just inside the cafeteria doors, walked over to Chet. She seemed a lot cheerier than she had the last time they'd seen her. She scowled at Pete's back. "Don't let Pete bug you," she told Chet. "He's just trying to psych out the competition."

"Right now," Chet said, an air of resignation in his voice, "I'm no competition to anyone."

"Have you looked for replacement cards on the Internet?" Daphne asked.

Chet shook his head. "Not yet," he said. "I was

53

thinking of doing that tonight, but I still haven't found a really good local site."

"You might try the Black Knight's site," Daphne said. "I've heard that Pete gets a lot of his best cards there."

"What about you?" Frank asked, stepping in. "Is that how you're rebuilding?"

"Nah," Daphne said. "I've got my own secrets. Good luck, Chet. You're going to need it to be ready by Tuesday."

"Thanks, Daphne," Chet said.

She started to go back inside the cafeteria, then turned and called back, "Remember, Chet, go where you gotta go to win."

"That's pretty ruthless," Iola said quietly, once Daphne had gone.

"I'm just glad she's bounced back from her loss," Chet said.

"You said she was one of the best players in town," Joe added. "Probably she's rebuilt her deck enough to feel confident again."

Frank rubbed his chin thoughtfully. "In any case, we'd better get going on Chet's posters," he said.

The others agreed and spent the rest of the lunch period plastering the halls with Chet's flyers.

At the end of the school day, the five of them met next to Chet's locker.

"Any news, Chet?" Callie asked.

Chet shook his head. "Not yet," he said. "I'm still hopeful, though."

"Did you catch up with Gerry?" Iola asked Frank and Joe.

"Nope," Joe said. "We talked to a lot of kids, but that guy is hard to find."

"Unless you're a buyer," Chet put in.

"We can phone Gerry tonight," Frank said. "I'm sure he knows about the theft—it's all over school. We just have to tell him what cards to watch out for."

"Besides, if he's such a shark at buying and selling, maybe we can get some tips from him on who might handle hot cards," Joe said.

"You think he deals stolen cards?" Callie asked.

"No," Frank said. "But with so much trading going on, he might be able to tell us who's trustworthy and who's not."

"You want to hit the ice-cream shop and get some sugar to jump-start our brains?" Chet suggested

"Sounds good," Joe said.

"No ice cream for me, though," Iola put in. "I don't care how warm it is out, I'm still feeling cold inside." She hugged her thick coat around herself and shivered to make the point.

"Yeah, okay," Chet said, laughing. "No ice cream for you. What about a nice hot chocolate? Just let me get my coat."

He opened his locker and a piece of folded white notebook paper fluttered to the floor.

"Fan mail?" Joe asked jokingly.

Chet picked up the paper and read it. The note was printed in plain, block lettering. It said:

Looking to replace your cards? Be at the north entrance of the deserted Benson Mini-Mall at 10 P.M. tonight. Don't bring a car. The parking lot is a mess. Any cars out front might be towed. There's no street parking, either. Hoof it or bike it or whatever. Come alone. Bring your cards and your cash.

7 Dangerous Game

"I don't like this, Chet," Frank said. "No cars? Come alone?"

"Frank's right," Joe said. "It sounds like a setup."

"That's why I won't be going alone," Chet said, smiling at the brothers.

"Chet, you don't mean . . ." Iola began.

"Hey," Chet said, "Frank and Joe know how to tail someone without being seen. Imagine how easy it'll be to keep *me* in sight."

Callie frowned. "It could still be dangerous," she said. "Maybe Iola and I should go, too."

"When tailing someone," Joe said, "I'm afraid two is company and four would be a crowd."

"You could wait a couple of blocks away in the van, if you want," Frank said. "We could keep in touch by cell phone."

"And we can come in blazing like the cavalry if you need us," Iola said, smiling.

Callie frowned. "Sitting in the van isn't my idea of exciting," she said.

Frank gave her hand a reassuring squeeze. "Detective work is like war," he said. "It's long periods of boredom followed by short bursts of intense action."

Callie folded her arms across her chest and scowled playfully at him. "I think that 'intense fear' is the original quote," she said.

"We'll leave the research to you, Callie," Joe said, smiling.

Callie sighed. "I'll have plenty of time for it," she said.

"We *both* will," Iola added.

"Let's head for home instead of getting ice cream," Frank suggested. "I want to have time to prepare for tonight."

The others nodded their agreement.

"I'll try to check the Internet, too," Chet said. "Maybe find that site Daphne mentioned."

"Good idea," said Joe. "Though I doubt you'll have time to pick up any cards tonight."

"I need to get some replacements soon," Chet said, "or I'm sunk."

They gathered at Chet and Iola's house just before nine. The Hardys arrived with Callie in their van. Callie brought a cell phone in order to keep in touch with the brothers. Looking at a map of the area, they picked a spot for the girls to wait with the van. Then they loaded Chet's bike into the back; the brothers had put their bikes in earlier.

"Why not just walk from where we park?" Callie asked. "There's a trail through the woods behind the mall. It cuts over into Magus Hills, a subdivision that's close to where we'll be waiting. I used to jog down that path all the time before the mall closed."

"I'd rather not walk an unfamiliar route at night if we don't have to," Frank said.

"Me, either," Chet added.

"Besides," Joe said, "we might need quicker transportation if something goes wrong."

Callie and Iola glanced uneasily at each other, but neither said anything.

"Let's roll," Frank said.

They piled into the van and soon they arrived at their parking spot: a small park about a half-mile from the mini-mall.

"We'll call you once we've got the place under surveillance," Joe said as he and the others got their bikes out of the back of the van.

"Good luck," Iola said, planting a kiss on Joe's cheek. She turned to Chet. "Take care of yourself, big brother."

Chet smiled confidently. "Don't worry. We're the Team Supreme."

"Keep the bike headlight on all the way, Chet," Frank said. "Joe and I will cut ours off at the top of the curve just south of the mall. We'll hang back far enough not to be seen when you arrive. Take your time getting to the north entrance, so we can get into position."

"If you need help," Joe said, "yell and we'll come flying."

"Check," Chet said.

"You guys remember to call if you need help, too," Callie cautioned.

"Don't worry," Joe replied. "None of us is about to get hurt over a deck of cards. We'll holler real loud if the plan goes south."

With a final goodbye, Joe, Frank, and Chet got on their bikes and were quickly out of sight.

The Benson Mini-Mall was in an older section of Bayport. It was one of many such malls that had sprouted up in the mid-1970s only to die from lack of business during the recession of the early '90s. It sat on a hillside, surrounded by woods and sleepy subdivisions. Below the mall lay the waterfront, above it the affluent neighborhoods of Bayport.

When they reached the sloping curve just south of the mall, Frank and Joe hit their brakes to let Chet build a comfortable lead on them. The brothers switched off their headlights. Friday night traffic was light, and there was little danger from oncoming cars.

When the Hardys rounded the curve, they spotted Chet pedaling hard across the cracked and broken asphalt parking lot. The mall lights were dark, but a three-quarter moon shown through a light cloud cover. The night was warm, and mist clung to the trunks of the trees dotting the hills that surrounded the mall.

Chet dismounted and walked his bike past the boarded-up mall toward the north entrance, on the far side of the parking lot.

"Let's cut to the left and circle around back," Joe suggested. "There's a service road behind the mall, and we can use the woods back there for cover."

"Right," Frank said. He and Joe kept to the shadows skirting the south edge of the lot. They wove across the battered pavement, dodging the dried weeds sprouting up through the cracks in the asphalt.

"I see why they said not to bring a car," Frank said in a low voice. "The lot is littered with broken glass."

"Looks like a recycling center waiting to happen," Joe agreed.

They pulled around the back of the mall and onto the service road. Recent rains had left a wide puddle running across the center of the access lane. A fallen birch tree blocked the road near the center of the mall.

Joe's eyes followed the ridge behind the building. "I think I see the path that Callie mentioned," he said, indicating an opening in the woods.

Frank nodded. "Nice to know about, even if we don't use it," he said. "Let's find Chet and then call the girls. You've got the cell phone?"

"At the ready," Joe said, patting his pocket.

They passed numerous doors on their way north. Many of the portals, like the windows out front, had been boarded over. Some, though, were bolted shut by heavy security locks.

Just before they reached the north entrance, the brothers noticed a half-dozen bicycles chained to trees. They also spotted three motorbikes and an ATV, locked to lampposts nearby.

"Looks like a regular convention," Joe whispered.

Frank nodded. "Let's cut upslope into the trees," he said.

The Hardys did so, and a minute later they had the north entrance to the mall in sight. One of the entryway's doors stood open and dim light leaked out from inside.

A figure dressed in a black monk's robe stood by the door. He had his hood pulled up over his head so that, even using the binoculars they'd brought, neither Frank nor Joe recognized him. The brothers watched quietly as Chet approached the door.

"Hey, Chet-man," the hooded figure said, the night air carrying his words to where the brothers sat hidden. "Glad you could make it. Chain your bike to a tree out back and come on in. Did you bring your money and any cards you have left?"

"I brought them," Chet said, looking a bit nervous. "But I still don't know what I brought them for."

"The *big game*, Chet," the figure said. "Boy, I thought you knew." The monk pulled his hood back to reveal his face in the dim light from the doorway. It was Gerry Wise. He smiled broadly. "We do this nearly every month," Gerry said. "Admission's fifteen bucks."

"Admission to what?" Chet asked.

Gerry laughed. "You really are out of the loop," he said. "It's a *keeper* game. People come from all over the county to play. You put your deck up against someone else's, and the winner gets his pick of cards from the other's deck."

Chet nodded uneasily.

"I've heard of this kind of game," Joe whispered to Frank. "Chet probably doesn't have the cards to compete in this."

"Gerry," Chet said, "you know my deck got swiped. I really don't have any good cards."

"Well, you're in luck, Chet-man," Gerry said. "Minimum to play is three cards worth ten dollars each— and I just happen to have a small selection with me. So, for only forty-five, including admission, you can buy yourself a seat at the game."

"Okay. I'm in," Chet said. He pulled the money out of his pocket and handed it to Gerry.

"Great," Gerry said. He reached into his robe and searched around a bit. "How about I set you up with the Samurai Scorpion, the Fiery Phoenix, and the Rogue Lion?" he said. "I'm giving you a bargain on price there. Will those three fit in with your deck?"

"Yeah," Chet said, nodding.

Gerry handed him the cards and something that looked like a crumpled-up wig.

Chet unfolded the wig and held it out in front of

him. It was a cheap rubber gorilla mask. "What's this for?" he asked.

"Most of the players at these games don't want to be recognized—it might hurt their tournament play," Gerry said. "So I provide disguises. Do you like my outfit? I'm the Mystic Monk."

"Yeah, okay," Chet said. "Isn't this all a bit melodramatic?"

"Hey!" Gerry said, throwing his arms wide. "This is Creature Cards—a world of magic and imagination. Loosen up, Chet-man. Go on inside. Follow the lights to the game area and deal yourself in."

Chet shot a final skeptical glance at Gerry. Then he chained up his bike and went inside. After Chet left, Gerry pulled a wad of cash out of his robes and began to count it.

"Come on," Frank whispered to Joe. "Let's sneak inside."

The brothers cut back to one of the doors they'd noticed earlier. Joe updated the girls while Frank picked the lock.

The Hardys crept through an empty storage room and a deserted store before coming to the mall's central walkway. Benson's Mini-Mall wasn't in much better shape inside than outside. Ceiling tiles and old electrical fixtures dangled haphazardly. The carpeting stank of mold, and the sound of dripping water echoed through the empty halls.

Peering out of the storefront window, the brothers saw a dozen people gathered around a sunken seating area in what had once been the center of the mini-mall. A circle of drop-lights ringed the playing pit. Most of the players wore strange masks and bulky clothing, to better hide their identities.

The contestants sat huddled in small groups, ranging from two to five people. The players talked animatedly as they laid their cards out, attacking and counterattacking. Chet, seated with four other players, was studying his situation carefully. A demon-masked player in a black satin jacket laughed as he laid down a winning card.

The Hardys crept closer to the game, trying to get a better look at the action. They stuck to the shadows and moved quietly so that the players wouldn't spot them.

"Recognize anyone?" Frank whispered.

Joe shook his head. "Not in those get-ups. The masks muffle their voices, too. If we hadn't seen Chet go in, I might not have recognized *him.*"

The competition grew intense. The smaller games died away, and soon there was one seven-person game left, with everyone else watching. Through clever play and perseverance, Chet had kept himself in the match.

Others in the group included the demon-masked man, a woman in a leather motorcycle jacket wearing a skeleton head, a vampire, an alien amazon, a rubber-faced ex-president, and a thin blond man in a blue down vest who wore no mask at all.

The blond man, who seemed just a few years older than the Hardys, looked at the demon player and laid a card down. "My DireWurm will aid the Samurai

Scorpion and join the siege against your Onyx Castle." He sat back and smiled, obviously pleased with his play.

Everyone sat silently for a moment while the demon-masked man pulled a card from the top of his deck and added it to his hand. He chuckled. "Looks like you're all out of luck, then," the demon said. "Because my Scarlet Sorceress is summoning up my Bargeist."

The players watching the game gasped at the bold move. "Fold up your decks," the demon-masked man said, "this game is mine." He took the Bargeist card from his hand and laid it out on the ground.

Before he could let it go, Chet reached out and grabbed the demon's wrist.

"I want to see that card," Chet said, his emotions almost visible.

"Back off, ape-boy," the demon man said coldly. He tried to pull his hand out of Chet's, but as he did so, a card slipped out of his sleeve and fell faceup on the ground.

"A Titanium Titan," the skull-faced woman said.

"This guy's been cheating!" Chet gasped.

8 Race in the Dark

"Give me that card!" Chet shouted.

The demon responded by punching Chet in the face.

Chet staggered back and tripped on a step leading down into the seating area.

Suddenly the room sprang to life as players dove to retrieve their cards. Chet lurched to his feet and lunged for the demon-masked man. The demon shoved the skull-faced woman into Chet. Chet tripped into the ex-president gamer and all three of them fell to the ground.

"Time to step in," Joe said. He and Frank leaped out from the storefront and sprinted toward the frenzied mob.

The gamers continued to tussle around the conversation pit. Some were already fleeing the scene, their precious cards clutched in their hands. Gerry came running from the north entrance yelling. "What's going on, man? Have you guys all gone crazy?" His black robes flew out behind him like a cape, but he didn't look at all heroic.

Gerry got to the melee at the same time the Hardys did. Chet was still tangled up with the ex-president and the skull-masked woman. His cards lay strewn around him. The vampire tripped and fell into the pile. The other players began scrambling for the nearest exit.

The demon-faced player and the blond man held each other in a clinch. Joe stepped forward to pull the two of them apart; Frank went to help Chet.

Chet staggered to his feet as the skull-woman sprang up and ran for an emergency exit. The vampire and the ex-president did the same.

"Are you all right?" Frank asked, steadying his friend.

Chet nodded groggily. "Just got the wind knocked out of me is all," he said.

The demon man spun as Joe reached for him, and the younger Hardy grabbed the blond man instead of his intended target. The man without a mask clouted Joe on the jaw. Joe rocked back and, as he did so, the demon sprinted toward him.

The demon-masked player hit Joe in the gut with his shoulder. The younger Hardy staggered, and his feet got tangled up with the blond man's legs. They both tumbled to the floor.

"Who're *you*?" the man cried. "You weren't in the game!"

"Frank! Chet!" Joe yelled from the floor, "The demon guy's getting away." He rolled away from the man—who no longer seemed interested in fighting—and got to his feet.

"I've got to pick up my cards," Chet said forlornly. He pulled off his gorilla mask and looked around at his scattered back-up deck.

"Don't worry, Chet," Frank called. "We're here to help."

Joe tossed the cell phone to Chet. Chet caught it and stooped to retrieve his cards. He was the only player left in the mall; even Gerry had vanished.

"Call your sister and Callie," Joe said. "Tell them what's going on and have them pick you up. With luck, we'll tackle that guy outside. If not, we'll get in touch when we can."

The Hardys ran for the exit just as the demon-masked player shoved his way out the door. The brothers flew after him into the night. It took a moment for their eyes to adjust to the darkness. Fog had sprung up while they were inside, and wisps of it danced like a parade of white ghosts through the moonlit trees. The brothers heard engines roaring nearby.

"Man," Joe said, "I hope that demon guy isn't on one of those motorcycles!"

Masked Creature Card players milled around, hopping onto their bicycles and taking off. The former president rocketed past the Hardys on a pair of in-line skates. None of the people nearby was the demon-faced man.

"Look!" Frank cried.

He pointed to two motorcycles and an ATV racing over the top of the wooded hill and on to Callie's trail. All the riders were wearing black jackets—just as the demon man had. Their helmets completely concealed their features. The empty demon mask dangled from a tree just beyond the flooded service road.

At that distance the Hardys couldn't tell which rider might be their quarry. Frank and Joe sprinted to their bikes.

"Good thing we've got our bad weather mountain tires on," Joe said as they took off after the riders. "If we pedal hard, we might just catch them."

"Assuming they don't know the trail any better than we do," Frank said grimly.

The brothers pedaled rapidly up the hill. When they reached the top, they spotted the lights of one motorcycle and the ATV racing down a ravine away from them. The other cycle had vanished.

"Think one of those is him?" Joe asked.

"We've got a two out of three chance," Frank replied. "And we're not giving up now!" He shot down the hill, his bike bouncing over rocks, roots, and fallen branches. Joe zipped after him.

The rough terrain took some of the advantage away from the ATV and the motorcycle. Because of their greater weight, the machines lurched and bounced more than the Hardys' bikes did. Obviously, neither of the riders was an expert on rough terrain. They skidded and sputtered their way up and down the hills.

Frank and Joe, on the other hand, had plenty of experience at both motocross and mountain bike races. The Hardys pumped up the hills with ease, and skidded down leaf-covered slopes without mishap. They rocketed across a small stream in their path, and dodged around tree stumps and other obstacles that suddenly loomed up out of the moonlit mist.

The brothers gained a lot of ground on the two riders. Both vehicles were sticking together—at least for the moment. The Hardys reached the bottom of a small gully just as the riders crested the next hill.

The Hardys shot after them. They topped the hill in no time and saw a sprawling subdivision in the rolling valley below. The riders skidded down the slope just a short distance ahead of the brothers.

"This must be Magus Hills—the neighborhood Callie mentioned," Frank called, without slacking his pace.

"If we had the cell phone, we could tell the girls to cut those riders off," Joe said.

"We'll just have to do the best we can on our own," Frank replied.

A large swath of hilly space wound between the large, expensive houses of Magus Hills. A pond sat in the middle of the subdivision, and a three-foot-wide creek meandered out of the pond and flowed into the distance. Cheery light streamed out of the houses into the dancing silver fog.

During the chase, the woods and mist had effectively hidden the Hardys from their quarry. Now the riders spotted Frank and Joe and both accelerated. It was all the brothers could do to keep up.

"Looks like they're in more familiar territory now," Joe said, panting.

Frank nodded and redoubled his efforts. Bumping over the open space, they weren't losing much ground, but they weren't gaining any, either. "Should we switch on our headlights?" he asked his brother.

"No," Joe replied. "We're doing okay without them. At this point they'd only ruin our night vision."

The ATV and the cycle nearly skidded out near a large two-story neo-Victorian. The backyard lights flicked on automatically, and a commotion rose up in the home. Unfortunately, the riders darted out of the light before the Hardys could recognize them.

Suddenly the motorcycle switched off its lights. A few seconds later, the ATV did the same.

"They must have figured the lights made them easier to follow," Joe said.

"Or easier to identify," Frank agreed. His breath came in heavy gasps, and his muscles ached, but he refused to quit.

The brothers had gained on their quarry during the skid out. Now only fifty yards separated them. The winding, landscaped terrain of the open space largely negated the superior horsepower of the motor vehicles.

All at once, though, a footbridge rose up on the left. The motorcyclist swerved and darted over the bridge as the Hardys whizzed past.

"Lost him!" Joe said. "That cyclist must have known that bridge was coming."

"Stay with the ATV," Frank called as the cycle disappeared into the fog. "It's two against one, now, and his rig is clumsy on this landscape."

"I don't have much left," Joe said, gasping. "But maybe we can outflank him somehow."

"Cut over that way," Frank said. "I'll try to chase him around the other side."

The flat grassy area they were riding over wound right. Joe cut left, pressing up over the top of a ten-foot-high hill. At the top of the hill, two tree trunks suddenly appeared out of the fog right in front of Joe.

Frank put on a final burst of speed and closed the distance on the ATV.

The rider glanced back over his shoulder. He spotted Frank and swerved left. Frank followed.

Joe darted between the trees, barely missing the trunks with his wide shoulders. As Joe topped the rise, the ATV skidded with Frank in hot pursuit. The four-wheeler was trapped between the brothers and a large pond. Joe barreled down the slope, switching on his headlight, and angling straight for the ATV.

The headlight surprised the rider, and he swerved

suddenly to the right. The ATV's tires skidded on the fog-slick grass and it went into a spin.

Joe clamped down on his brakes, but the tires didn't catch. He slid toward the spinning four-wheeler, unable to stop. Frank, too, skidded headlong toward the impending pileup. Both Hardys braced themselves for a spectacular three-way crash.

9 Networking

At the last instant Joe leaped off his bike. He flew over the spinning tires and landed on the rider of the ATV. The rider's breath *wooshed* out as both he and Joe fell to the ground.

Frank kept skidding toward the ATV. Desperate, he leaned over the handlebars and spun his bike on the front wheel. The rear of the bike whipped around and hit the four-wheeler. The collision threw Frank over his handlebars.

The elder Hardy tucked into a forward roll, hoping to blunt the impact as he crashed. He landed hard on Joe and the ATV rider, cracking his elbow on the rider's helmet. The three of them tumbled down the side of the pond, stopping two feet before the water's edge. Riderless, the ATV rolled down into the pond and sputtered to a stop.

Joe and Frank lay stunned for a moment. The ATV rider groaned.

"Are you okay?" Joe finally asked.

"Yeah," Frank replied. He felt woozy, but the spots had begun to clear from his eyes. "How about you?"

"I've been better," Joe said. "At least we caught the guy we were after."

Frank and Joe disentangled themselves from the rider and rolled slowly to either side. "Do you think he's all right?" Frank asked.

Joe dragged himself into a sitting position. At the same time, the rider groaned again. "He's alive, at least," Joe said.

Despite the pain in his elbow, Frank sat up. The rider sat up as well.

"Are you guys crazy?" asked a muffled voice from inside the helmet. "Man, does my head hurt!" He pulled the helmet off and set it on the grass beside him. The face under the helmet belonged to Gerry Wise.

Frank's and Joe's hearts sank. They'd caught the wrong man.

As the bad news sank in, lights from a police cruiser appeared on the far side of the pond. A voice coming over a loudspeaker said:

"All of you, stay right where you are!"

Joe and Frank knew the Bayport Police Headquarters well. They'd been there many times while working on cases. Usually, though, they came as visitors, not suspects.

The brothers sat in a holding area while the police worked out the details of what had happened. Finally, their friend Officer Con Riley came over to see them.

"Well," he said, "this is a bigger mess than you're usually in." Con often lent them a sympathetic ear when they were working on a case.

"It seemed like a good idea at the time," Frank said, rubbing his sore elbow.

Con shook his head disapprovingly. "Right now I think the best idea would be for you boys to go home and get some rest."

"We're not being charged with anything?" Joe asked, a trace of surprise in his voice.

"Luckily for you, no," Con said. "Gerry Wise lives in the Magus Hills subdivision. His father built that entire tract of houses. Gerry has a right to use the recreational space as he sees fit. That use may *not* include racing around on a four-wheeler in the pitch-dark with his friends—but that's a matter for the neighborhood association. Probably, they'll fine him and make him clean up the damage. I've a feeling that you boys might like to help out on that front."

Frank nodded, but Joe blurted out, "He was running a shady card game in the old Benson Mini-Mall."

Con folded his arms across his chest and nodded in return. "Yup. I know all about that. Your friend's father owns that building. Gerry had permission to run games there—though I gather that tonight's affair got a little out of hand."

"You might say that," Joe said, rubbing his ribs where the demon-masked man had hit him.

"As to the game itself . . ." Con shrugged. "I don't pretend to understand this collector card stuff. What they were doing sounds like it *might* be gambling, but we don't have anything solid to hang a charge on—despite what you saw. I'm not sure you'd want us to do that anyway. Probably some of those players are friends of yours." Con shot the brothers a look that said he knew they'd followed someone there, though both Hardys had kept Chet's name out of their statements.

"You might be right," Frank said.

"It was hard to tell with everyone wearing masks," Joe added.

"So, go on, get out of here," Con said, waving his hand toward the door.

"Thanks, Con," Frank said.

"Don't thank me," the officer said. "Just thank your lucky stars that Chief Collig isn't on duty tonight. You know how much he 'likes' both of you." Con grinned.

The Hardys smiled back and headed out of the holding room. In the foyer, they met their father, Fenton Hardy, as well as Chet, Iola, and Callie.

"Sorry we got you out of bed for nothing, Dad," Joe said.

"I'm glad they're not charging you," Mr. Hardy said, "and I'm glad that you're both safe. On the whole, though, I would have preferred a good night's sleep."

"I couldn't have slept anyway, until I heard from

Joe," Iola said. Joe gave her a quick, reassuring hug. Frank did the same for Callie.

"Did you recover all the cards you brought to the game, Chet?" Frank asked.

"Yeah. Some of them got a bit stomped, but they're all there and usable," Chet replied.

"I don't know about the rest of you," Callie said, "but I'm beat. And I'm *very* glad tomorrow is Saturday and we don't have school."

"I've still got a lot of work to do," Chet said, "to get ready for the tournament on Tuesday."

"And I'm betting our bikes need some work as well," Joe said, sighing.

"I think you can sort all that out in the morning," Mr. Hardy said. "That is, if any of you are up before noon."

The whole group chuckled and headed for the door. They ran into Gerry Wise and his father, who were leaving at the same time. Mr. Wise scowled at the Hardys.

Gerry grinned sheepishly at the brothers. "Sorry about this, guys," he said. "It was all just a big misunderstanding. I'm glad nobody really got hurt."

"Us, too," Frank said. "We'll lend you a hand repairing any damage."

"I'll say you will," Mr. Wise said angrily. "You're lucky we don't have you boys up for assault!"

"Hey, cool it, Dad," Gerry said.

"I think the kids can settle this on their own," Mr. Hardy said calmly. "There's nothing that a few apologies and some elbow grease can't fix."

Mr. Wise frowned but didn't say anything more.

As they all walked down the front steps, Gerry hung back with the others and whispered, "Chet, I hope you'll play next month. This kind of stuff doesn't usually happen."

"I can't believe that you'd—" Joe began.

Frank cut him off. "Gerry, did you know all the players at the game?"

"Most of them, yeah," Gerry said.

"And you supplied the masks?" Frank asked.

"Most of them," Gerry repeated.

"So, who was the demon-masked guy who started all the trouble?" Joe asked.

Gerry shrugged. "I don't know," he said. "Some of the players wear their own masks when they show up. They don't want *anyone* guessing who they are. That way, their card strategies remain a complete secret."

"Too bad," Joe muttered.

Gerry waved goodbye and got into his father's limo. The teens piled into the Hardys' van, and Fenton Hardy went to his own car.

"Come straight home as soon as you've dropped everyone off," Fenton said to his sons.

Joe and Frank nodded. "Don't worry, Dad," Joe said. "The only place we're going tonight is to bed."

Frank and Joe did get up before noon, but not *much* before noon. They spent the remainder of Saturday morning working on their bikes, which their father had reclaimed from the police. The bicycles were pretty badly beaten up.

Chet Morton showed up around one with Iola and Callie.

"Hey, guys," Chet said. "How's it going?"

"We've had better mornings," Joe said, wiping the sweat from his brow with a grease-stained towel. He cleaned his hands on the towel and said, "Hi, Callie. Hi, Iola."

"Chet's been pacing around like a caged lion all morning," Iola said.

Chet sighed with frustration. "I'm out forty-five bucks," he said, "and I'm not much closer to having my deck rebuilt."

"What about that Internet site Daphne mentioned?" Frank asked.

"I used most of the search engines available, but I couldn't find it," Chet said forlornly. "Every time I typed in 'Black Knight,' I kept coming up with role-playing game sites."

Frank wiped the bicycle grease from his hands. "Maybe we should ask Daphne to show us the site personally."

"Good idea," Joe said.

"Iola and I did some checking this morning," Callie said. "It turns out that Gerry, Daphne, and Pete all live in that same subdivision."

Frank gave his girlfriend a kiss on the cheek. "Not only beautiful, but smart, too."

"So either Pete or Daphne could have been the cyclist we chased into Magus Hills," Joe said. "I've seen them both riding motorcycles, too."

81

"I don't think Daphne could have been the demon-masked guy, though—not unless she's an Oscar-winning makeup artist," Chet said.

"Pete looks like our best bet," Frank said, "but there may be other suspects we haven't considered."

"Well," Joe said, "until we get more evidence, I think we should take Frank's suggestion and talk to Daphne."

All of them agreed, and after the Hardys showered, they all hopped into the van and headed for Daphne's house—a new, two-story colonial on Hebert Avenue. Daphne answered the door when they rang the bell.

"Hey, guys," she said pleasantly, "this must be my day for friends dropping in unexpectedly."

"Who else has dropped by?" Frank asked.

"Tim showed up earlier," she said. "We were going to have a tune-up game, but the big dummy left his cards in his school locker. He was going to try and get them."

"Getting his deck from school on a Saturday?" Chet said skeptically.

"There's a volleyball game in the gym today," Callie said. "He *might* be able to get in."

Daphne shrugged. "I haven't seen him since, so who knows? What can I do for you guys? Did you come to get humiliated in a tune-up game, Chet?"

Chet shook his head. "Nope," he said. "My deck's still pretty sparse."

"Still?" Daphne said, raising her eyebrows. "Get it together, Morton. You'll never make it past the first round of the tourney this way."

"I know," Chet said. "That's why we came to see

you. I tried to find the Black Knight site, but I didn't have any luck."

Daphne gently slapped her forehead. "I'm sorry. I should have sent you the URL. Come on in. We'll send an instant message from my machine to the Knight. You can pick up the conversation at your place later."

"Good idea," Chet said.

Daphne led the teens into her house. "Mom," she called to an unseen parent, "I've got some friends over to surf the Net."

"That's fine, dear" came a reply from the other room.

Chet and the others went upstairs to Daphne's room. There they found the latest in computer equipment as well as the usual posters and memorabilia.

Daphne quickly logged on to the Net.

"The site is kind of hidden," Daphne explained. "You can't find it unless someone shows you. There. I've E-mailed the URL to you, Chet."

"Thanks," Chet said. He stood next to Daphne; the rest of the group watched over their shoulders.

Daphne's fingers flew over the keyboard. In seconds the Black Knight's site appeared on the screen. It had a crude castle and a block-lettered title. As the page opened, a deep voice came over the monitor, "Halt! Who goes there?"

Daphne typed in her name and password. The doors to the castle opened, a new screen popped up, and the computer voice said, "Welcome, Lady Soesbee." Daphne moved her cursor across the new screen and pressed the Send a Message option.

She requested that the Black Knight contact Chet at his home E-mail address as soon as possible. She stressed that Chet needed to buy cards before Tuesday's tournament. Then she sat back and smiled with satisfaction.

"That's all there is to it?" Joe asked.

"Yep," Daphne said. As she spoke, a bell sounded and a new screen popped up on her monitor.

"It's from the Black Knight," Daphne said. "He must have been online when we wrote."

"Let's see what he has to say," Frank said.

Daphne pressed a few keys and the reply opened up. It read: "Lady Soesbee: Tell your friend to wait for my E-mail tonight. We'll set up a meeting.—The Black Knight"

10 The Black Knight

That evening the Hardys and their girlfriends sat in the Mortons' family room sipping sodas while Chet paced the floor.

"Chet," Iola said, "wearing out the carpet isn't going to make the Black Knight get back to you any earlier."

"I know," Chet replied, "but I can't think of anything else to do."

"Maybe you should go to the Dungeon Guild," Frank suggested. "You were going to see if you could pick up some cards there."

"Good idea," Callie said. "At least the Dungeon Guild owner operates out in the open."

"Well, kind of out in the open," Frank said. "Remember when we followed him to his secret park meeting."

"Mystery and imagination are part of the game," Chet replied. "A lot of players like that kind of thing."

"Right now, though," Joe said, "all the mystery is getting in the way. We're no closer to solving these card thefts than we were when we started."

Iola put a hand on his shoulder. "You and Chet should both calm down, Joe," she said. "Stewing about it won't help anything."

"Maybe Frank's right," Chet said. "I should check the Dungeon Guild before it closes. Anyone want to go with me?"

Before anyone could answer, the doorbell rang. Chet answered it and found Tim Lester waiting on the doorstep.

"Tim, hey," Chet said. "What brings you here?"

"I dug through my extra cards and found some that I thought you might be able to use," Tim said, holding out a big shoebox. "If you want them, you can have them for last month's prices."

Chet smiled. "Thanks, Tim. Come on in. The Hardys and Callie are hanging out, too." All of them said hi to Tim.

"Did you get your cards from school?" Joe asked.

Tim looked puzzled. "How'd you know about that?"

"Daphne clued us in," Frank said. "We saw her this afternoon."

Tim shook his head. "Nah. I couldn't get them. I left them in my locker after McCool almost busted us yesterday. Pretty stupid, eh? I got into the school, but the cops were hanging around, so I couldn't get close to my locker."

"The police?" Callie said. "Why were they at school?"

"I heard somebody stole a big camera from the industrial arts room," Tim said, "but I don't know for sure. Anyway, I couldn't get my deck. At least with the cops around, my best cards should be safe."

"Unless the police start opening lockers," Chet said.

Tim's face fell. "You don't think they'd do that, do you?"

"They might," Joe said. "It depends on what they're looking for."

"Well, they can't be looking for Chet's cards, because he never reported them stolen," Iola said, frowning.

"You really have to do that, Chet," Callie added.

"Maybe later," Chet replied. He was already busy thumbing through Tim's shoebox.

Frank rubbed his chin. "Crime seems to be epidemic at Bayport High lately," he said. "I'll check with Con and find out what's going on."

"Go ahead," Chet said. "I'm going to see if Tim's got any cards I want. First, though, I've got to do something." Chet walked to the family computer sitting in one corner of the room.

"Chet, you just checked ten minutes ago," Iola complained.

"Yeah, I know, but . . ." Chet said. He typed some commands in and then was frustrated when nothing was there.

"Why don't I set the program to ring when new mail comes in?" Callie suggested.

"Good idea," Joe said. "That way, maybe Chet can

87

keep his blood pressure from blowing off the top of his head."

Callie and Iola worked on the computer while Chet and Tim riffled through Tim's cards. Frank and Joe went outside to talk to Con Riley on their cell phone.

Half an hour later they regrouped in the family room. Chet appeared much happier, as did Tim—who was counting his new-found money. The girls were sitting on the couch, chatting.

"Computer all set?" Joe asked.

Callie nodded. "Fired up and ready to sing out," she said.

"My deck's in a little better shape," Chet said. "Though I still need some powerful cards to make a decent bid at the tournament."

"My wallet's fatter," Tim said, smiling. "And that's a good thing."

"What did Con have to say?" Iola asked.

"The theft at the school had nothing to do with cards," Frank said. "Tim was almost right. It wasn't a camera that was missing, though, just a lens."

"For the separations camera used in Mr. McCool's class," Joe added. "One of the students using the lab after school on Friday reported the theft."

Tim breathed a sigh of relief. "At least the cops won't be busting me for having cards in my locker," he said.

The others chuckled.

Tim stood. "I hate to take the money and run," he said, "but I should get going."

"Maybe you could drop by tomorrow for a tune-up game," Chet suggested. "I could invite Daphne, too."

"Sounds great," Tim replied as he stepped out the door. "Bye!"

Joe sat down on the couch next to Iola. "Maybe we could talk to Daphne if she drops by tomorrow," he said.

"It might be that Daphne and Chet's thefts are unrelated," Frank said. "The cards *are* valuable. Maybe we're looking at crimes of opportunity here."

"But it's not just Daphne and me," Chet said. "Other people have lost individual cards. And why is all this happening just now?"

"The cards have gotten a lot more popular lately," Iola said. "I'd never even heard of them until you got serious about the game, Chet."

"Too bad you tussled with Gerry last night," Callie said to the Hardys. "Maybe he could have tipped you to some places to look for the crooks."

"Yeah," Joe said. "We should try him. He didn't seem to hold the mistake against us."

"Holding grudges is bad business," Chet interjected.

"We'll chat with Gerry in the next day or two," Frank said, "once things cool down. I'm still hoping he can tell us something the other kids didn't."

"There are only three days until Chet's tournament," Iola said. "That doesn't leave you much time."

"We can handle the pressure," Joe said, leaning his head back and closing his eyes.

Chet chuckled. "I'm getting a soda," he said. "Anybody else want one?"

89

"Sure," the others chimed together.

Chet returned a few minutes later with five cans of soda, a big bag of tortilla chips, and a bowl of salsa. As he entered the room, the bell on the computer rang out.

Chet nearly dropped the snacks in his dash for the keyboard. The others got off the couch and came to peer over Chet's shoulder.

"It's a message from the Black Knight," Chet said. "He says I can meet him at midnight tonight at the seven-mile marker on Old Bluff Road. He says I should come alone."

"That's not too far from Magus Hills," Callie noted.

Joe and Frank glanced at each other, remembering that Pete, Daphne, and Gerry all lived in that subdivision.

"What is it with these guys and their mysterious meetings?" Iola asked rhetorically.

Frank checked his watch. "We don't have a lot of time to get there and set up," he said.

"It's almost two hours until midnight," Iola replied, puzzled.

"Yeah, but we need to get there early enough so the Knight won't know we've arrived first," Joe said. "We'll stake the place out, just in case Chet runs into trouble."

"We'll come along," Callie said.

Frank took her hand and squeezed it sympathetically. "Not this time, I'm afraid," he said.

"Too many detectives spoil the stakeout," Joe said,

finishing his brother's thought. He gave Iola a kiss on the cheek by way of consolation.

"So you expect us to wait here?" Iola asked.

"You could drive me out," Chet suggested, "but then you'd have to hide in the car or something."

"Just so long as we don't have to hide in the trunk," Callie said.

"*Again*," Iola added with a deadpan face.

The Hardys arrived at the meeting place on Old Bluff Road just before eleven o'clock. They parked in a culvert half a mile back and hiked up the ridge to the seven-mile marker.

The brothers found a concealed spot in the trees and sat down to wait. It was colder than it had been the night before, and much gloomier. Fog had sprung up again and, tonight, cloud cover blotted out the moonlight. Even after their eyes adjusted, the brothers couldn't see more than twenty feet in the darkness.

"I'm really getting sick of this fog," Joe said.

"When the weather turns cold again, it'll leave," Frank said.

Joe frowned. "That's a mixed blessing," he said. "Outside stakeouts are easier when the weather's like this."

"Pipe down," Frank whispered. "I think Chet's coming."

Sure enough, Chet's old sedan chugged up the hill and pulled onto the shoulder. Chet got out and stood by the side of the road.

Joe checked his watch. Five minutes to midnight. They waited.

Chet paced nervously, wearing small ruts into the gravel shoulder of the road. Fifteen minutes passed. Then thirty. Then forty-five.

After nearly an hour Chet whispered loudly, "Frank! Joe! I don't think he's coming."

The Hardys left their hiding place and walked downhill to Chet. Callie and Iola sat up in Chet's car.

"My neck is sooo stiff!" Callie complained.

"At least you were in the back," Iola said. "I've had the gearshift digging into my ribs all this time."

"Sorry about the waste of time, girls," Frank said. "Looks like we've washed out this time."

Chet sighed. "I was hoping to at least get a shot at some good cards," he said.

"You might get that chance yet," Joe said quietly. His eyes narrowed as he focused on some evergreen bushes just down the road. He turned back to Chet and Frank.

"What do you see, Joe?" Frank whispered.

"Somebody's lurking in those bushes," Joe said. "I saw his shadow move."

"Let's get him," Frank said. He and Joe turned and ran for the bushes at full speed.

The hiding figure jumped up and started skidding down the sloped side of Old Bluff Road. The fog and darkness made it impossible to determine the person's identity.

"We'll cut him off with the car!" Chet called after

the brothers. The Hardys heard Chet's car engine roar to life atop the bluff.

The fog obscured the brothers' vision, making their quarry difficult to follow. "Isn't Magus Hills down in this direction?" Joe called.

"I think so," Frank replied. "It's hard to tell in this fog. Whoever he is, this guy knows the terrain better than we do."

"Yeah," Joe said. "We'd have caught him by now otherwise."

The figure ahead of them darted to the right across the top of a ridge, hardly breaking stride even though the slope dropped away precipitously.

Joe and Frank sprinted to the top of the cliff after him, starting to close the gap slightly.

As they crested the ridge, though, the sandy ground crumbled beneath Frank's feet. He started a slide toward the edge of the cliff.

11 A Card Revealed

Frank reached out to grab on to Joe, but the younger Hardy's footing slipped as well. As Frank clutched Joe's coat, both of them slid standing up over the drop.

Their feet flew out from under them, spraying small stones and sand into the air. Clawing with their fingers, they caught the edge of the slope, and both slammed hard into the sandy cliffside.

"Oof!" Joe gasped. "You okay, Frank?"

"I've been better," Frank replied. "I don't have a very good grip."

"Neither do I," Joe said. "The sand on the cliff face keeps slipping out from under my feet."

Frank nodded. "Me, too. I've climbed ice walls that were easier to get purchase on."

The ledge under Joe's fingers crumbled and he slipped a few feet more before he could get a better grip and stop his descent. "I could use a rope right about now," he said grimly.

"Here! Catch my coat!" a voice called down from above.

A heavy maroon jacket dangled in front of the younger Hardy, and Joe grabbed it just as the surface gave way beneath him. The person holding the other end of the coat grunted as Joe's weight fell on him. Joe looked up and saw Pete Kaufmann grimacing with exertion.

"I—I don't know if I can pull you both up," Pete said.

"Help Joe," Frank replied. "I've got a better grip now."

Pete pulled, and Joe tried to help by scrambling with his feet—to no avail.

Chet Morton, sweating and panting, suddenly appeared beside Pete on top of the ridge. "Let me give you a hand," Chet said.

Together, they hauled Joe up first, and then got Frank.

"Boy, am I ever glad to see you!" Joe said to Chet.

"Yeah, thanks, Chet," Frank said. "You, too, Pete."

Pete sat down to catch his breath.

"Good thing I decided to follow on foot while the girls took the car," Chet said.

Frank pulled his cell phone from his pocket and handed it to Chet. "Call Callie's phone and tell the girls that we're all right," he said. "Joe and I want to chat with Pete."

Chet nodded grimly. "So, you're the Black Knight," he said to Pete.

"What? Me?" Pete sputtered. "I'm not the Black Knight."

"If you're not," Joe said, "what were you doing at the seven-mile marker on Old Bluff Road?"

"I always meet the Knight there," Pete said. "He suggested the spot the first time I contacted him. I got a note from him earlier tonight that said he had a good card for me and that I should show up at half-past midnight."

"What's he look like?" Joe asked.

"I've never seen his face," Pete replied. "He wears a motorcycle helmet and jacket. He's pretty tall, maybe about Joe's size."

Frank frowned. "A very convenient story."

"It's the truth!" Pete snapped. "When I saw Chet at the rendezvous point, I knew something was wrong. The Knight *never* meets two clients at once. When you guys appeared, I figured it was some kind of set-up. I thought that maybe you'd tapped into the Knight's E-mail and sent me a decoy note to throw off my game plan for Tuesday's tournament."

"Why'd you run?" Joe asked.

Pete shrugged. "There were five of you and one of me," he said. "How did I know what you were up to? I figured I'd lose you along the ridge. But I didn't think you'd fall off." He took a deep breath, stood, and dusted himself off. "I didn't *have* to come back for you, you know."

"We're glad you did," Frank said. "Thanks."

"Can I go now?" Pete asked.

Joe nodded. "Sure, take off," he said. "We might want to talk to you again, though."

"I'm in the phone book," Pete answered. He walked down the ridge and disappeared into the fog.

"I told the girls to meet us at the bottom of the hill," Chet said, handing the cell phone back to Frank. I figured it'd be easier than climbing back up."

"Good thinking," Joe said.

After returning to Chet's car, the Hardys told the others what they'd learned.

"The way I see it, there are two possibilities," Frank said. "One, that Pete really *is* the Black Knight, and what he told us was just a good cover story. Two, that the Knight spotted our stakeout and took off before Pete arrived."

"That doesn't explain Pete's presence, though," Joe said. "There's a third possibility, that the whole trip was a set-up—both for us and for Pete."

"But, why?" Iola asked.

Joe shook his head. "I don't know. Maybe the Knight is one of the other regular Creature Card players."

"*He* might even be *Daphne,*" Frank said. "She could have faked that reply from the Knight when we were at her house. None of us was really watching her."

"This is making my head hurt," Chet said. "All I wanted to do was win a card game."

"I'm sure we'll have a better take on it in the morning," Frank said.

They all went home, but the Hardys didn't sleep well. The puzzling facts of the case kept running through their heads.

The brothers arrived at Iola and Chet's house just after two on Sunday afternoon. Callie was there, too, as were Tim and Daphne. The girls, Chet, and Tim were deep into a game of Creature Cards.

"I thought you didn't know how to play," Joe said to Iola.

"It's easy to learn," Iola replied. "Chet and Tim taught us both this morning."

"Tim and I scraped together enough cards so they could play," Chet said. "And since we're only using basic decks, the odds are pretty even. It was a good chance to get in some group play before the tournament."

Tim smiled at Joe and Frank. "Your girlfriends are pretty good for beginners," he said.

"You guys gonna talk, or play?" Daphne asked, half-jokingly.

"Okay," Callie said, "I guess my Centaur Chief will attack Daphne's Goblin Militia."

"Then my White Knight will have to come to the Goblins' rescue," Daphne said, laying her defensive card down.

"Can you use a Knight to help the Goblins?" Iola asked.

Chet gasped. "That's my card!" he said, reaching across the table.

Joe grabbed his arm. "Slow down, Chet," he said. "You've overreacted to duplicate cards twice before."

This time, though, Chet maintained his calm. "No, really, that's the White Knight from my deck. See the ketchup stain in the corner?" he said, pointing to the upper right edge of the card. Sure enough, a faint red blotch discolored the corner.

"Where'd you get this card, Daphne?" Frank asked.

Both Tim and Daphne squirmed in their seats. "I won it from somebody," Daphne finally said.

"Someone at the game in the mall the other night?" Joe asked.

"Well . . . yeah," she said. "I was at that game. I won the card fair and square. Things were going well for me until that gorilla guy broke things up."

"Chet was that gorilla," Frank said. "Which mask were you wearing? The skull?"

"I'd rather not say," Daphne said. "Professional secret." She took the card off the table. "Look, Chet, if this is part of your stolen deck, you can have it back. It's just a common card anyway." She handed it to him.

"Thanks, Daphne," Chet said, taking the White Knight and smiling at her.

"You couldn't have rebuilt your deck just at that game, Daphne," Joe said. "How *did* you do it?"

Daphne stood up. "Look," she said, "I came here to play a friendly game, not to reveal my strategy and tactics."

"Well, would you take a look at the list of Chet's

stolen cards, and tell us if any of the others are in your deck?" Frank asked.

Daphne turned on her heel. "That's it!" she said angrily. "I'm out of here." She stormed out the door.

Tim, looking uncomfortable, got up as well. "I think maybe I'd better leave, too," he said, following Daphne out.

After Tim left, Iola said, "Wow. You'd think that you guys asked to read Daphne's diary or something."

"I know where she's coming from," Chet said. "She's really worried about that tournament, I think."

"I understand," Joe said, "but I'm not very sympathetic. We're trying to solve a series of crimes here."

"Maybe *she* stole Chet's cards," Callie suggested.

"It'd be pretty foolish to steal Chet's cards and then flaunt them in front of him," Frank said.

"Well, all the knight cards look alike," Iola said. "And Daphne said that she hadn't noticed the ketchup stain."

"Without the stain, who could tell that card was Chet's?" Callie asked excitedly. "Maybe Daphne's rebuilt her own deck by stealing Chet's and that's why she's in such good shape."

"Or, she could have bought new cards from Mr. Felix," offered Joe. "That's just as likely, I think."

Callie leaned her chin on her hands and sighed. "There are too many suspects in this case," she said. "Daphne . . . Pete . . . Gerry . . . even Tim. It could be any of them."

Chet got up and headed for the door.

"Where are you going, Chet?" Frank asked.

"Well, first I'm stopping by the police station to report my cards stolen," Chet said. "The cops may not take me seriously, but at least my complaint will be on the record. Then I'm going to hit the Dungeon Guild. I've tried the other ways I can think of. Getting the cards I need from Ron Felix seems like my best option at this point—even if it costs me big bucks."

"Want us to go with you?" Joe asked.

"No," Chet said. "I need to do this alone."

When he'd gone, Frank turned to the others and said, "I know we're doing our best, but I can't help feeling we've let him down."

"Maybe you guys should take the rest of the day off," suggested Callie. "After two late-night chases, you're too burned out to think straight. Let's go to a movie or something."

Frank and Joe nodded wearily. "Yeah," Joe said. "Maybe relaxing for a bit will help."

Unfortunately, going to the movies didn't take the Hardys' minds off their troubles. When they got home, they tried to reach Gerry, but only got his family's answering machine. Frank and Joe spent the evening going over the case, but none of the pieces fell into place.

The brothers met Chet, Iola, and Callie in the school parking lot Monday morning, and all five of them walked toward the school together.

A police cruiser, its engine still running, stood

parked outside the front entrance. Tim came bounding down the steps past the cruiser.

"You guys should see it!" he said. "Mr. McCool's really lighting into the cops!"

"What for?" Joe asked.

"I don't know," Tim said. "They're arguing by my locker. Check it out."

The Hardys and their friends picked their way through the students crowding the foyer and went to Tim's locker near the industrial arts room. Mr. McCool was standing outside the door to the classroom, holding a fist-size black box in his hand. Con Riley was talking with him. Another officer stood near the two, quietly staying out of the conversation.

"I can't believe all this lunacy!" McCool said, holding out the box. "This lens wasn't stolen. It's right here. I put it away for the weekend. There's no crime here, no mystery."

"According to the student who reported the incident, the lens wasn't where it was supposed to be," Con said calmly.

McCool blew out a long huff of air. "I'm sorry I didn't put it in the usual place," McCool said. "But here it is. You can see it with your own eyes. If anyone had called me, I could have told you where to find it."

"We tried to get in touch with you, Mr. McCool," Con said. "But we couldn't reach you all weekend."

"Is that my fault?" McCool asked. "I have to get ready for class. Is there anything else you need from me?"

102

Con tipped his hat back on his head. "No, sir. I think that'll do."

"Good," McCool said, stalking back into his classroom.

"What a hoot!" Tim said quietly. "Good thing the cops didn't find my cards. I've been worried about them all weekend." He took off his coat and opened his locker door.

A Creature Card fluttered out of Tim's locker and fell faceup on the floor.

Chet's eyes went wide and he gasped, "My Bargeist!"

12 The Tournament

Tim's jaw dropped. "H-How did *that* get in there?" he stammered. He looked up to find all eyes on him. "Hey," he said sheepishly, "you don't think I had anything to do with this."

"You're sure this is your card, Chet?" Joe asked.

Chet picked up the Bargeist and examined it.

"Well, it's not *mine!*" Tim put in defensively.

"I can't be sure," Chet said, his mouth drawn into a tight line. "But there aren't a lot of Bargesits in circulation. It's a very rare card. This *could* be the one from my missing deck."

At that moment Con Riley and the other officer walked by on their way to the front door. "What's that?" Con said. "You found one of your stolen cards?"

"The Bargeist," Iola interjected. "It's rare and very valuable."

"Where did it turn up?" Con asked.

"It fell out of my locker when I opened it," Tim said. "But I don't know how it got there."

"Really . . ." Con said, rubbing the slight stubble on his chin. The officer with Con glanced suspiciously at Tim. "What's your name, son?" Con asked.

"Tim Lester," Tim said, his voice shaking nervously. "But I really don't know anything about this. Honest, Officer Riley!"

"I think you and I should have a talk," Con said. He turned to his partner. "Officer Chisholm, please secure that locker until we can investigate further."

"Right," Officer Chisholm said. She closed Tim's locker and took up a position in front of the door. "The rest of you, move along," she said to the Hardys and their friends.

"But it's *my* cards that were stolen," Chet said.

"I know, that Chet," Con said. "For now, though, I'll have to ask you for that card. We may need it as evidence."

Reluctantly, Chet handed over the Bargeist. "Will I get it back in time for tomorrow's tournament?" Chet asked.

"We'll do our best," Con said. "I can't make any promises, though." He looked at the rest of the group. "You should get to class. I may need to talk to the rest of you, though. We'll be in touch. Keep an eye on that locker, Marge."

Officer Chisholm nodded. "Check. Tell Crime Scene to hurry back."

105

"Don't worry, I will," Con said. "Come on, Mr. Lester. We need to talk to the principal. After that, we'll go to the station and take your statement." Con headed for the principal's office with Tim meekly tagging along.

Other students had begun to gather around the locker, trying to find out the cause of the commotion. Officer Chisholm stared them down. "Move along," she said. "Nothing to see here." She spared a parting glance at Chet, the Hardys, and the girls. "You, too."

The brothers and their friends moved down the hall. "Why didn't you say anything?" Callie asked Frank and Joe.

"There wasn't much to say," Frank said. "We couldn't stop Con from doing his job."

"And we didn't want to say anything that might put Tim in more trouble than he already was in," Joe added.

"Do you think he could have done it?" Iola asked.

"He knew Chet's cards were in that desk," Frank said. "And he had both motive and opportunity to take them."

"A lot of other people knew that as well," Iola said. "Gerry told us all the gamers knew the cards were confiscated. Tim seems too nice to do something that rotten to Chet."

"I agree," Callie said. "And, if he did take that card, why put it in his locker, and why open the locker in front of us?"

"Criminals *do* make mistakes," Joe said. "That's usually why they're caught. I'll admit, though, it doesn't make much sense."

"I don't think either of us is ready to condemn Tim," Frank added. "But he *could* have done it."

"Then the only logical choice is that someone framed him for it," Callie said. "Someone like Pete or Daphne."

"Or someone we haven't even considered yet," Iola put in. "You're awfully quiet, Chet. What do you think?"

Chet sighed. "I'm almost wishing that I hadn't reported the theft to the cops. If I hadn't, maybe Frank and Joe could have handled this more quietly."

"It's a bad break," Frank said, "but reporting the theft was the right thing to do."

"I wonder if Daphne ever reported her loss," Joe mused. "If she didn't, that might indicate that she didn't want the police looking into the theft."

"Are you saying she might have faked the theft of her own cards?" Iola asked.

Joe shrugged. "It wouldn't be the first time a criminal has played the victim," he said.

"On the other hand," Frank said, "Pete's competition for tomorrow's tournament is looking pretty thin right now. Chet and Daphne had cards stolen, and now Tim is being investigated by the police. Even if all three of them make the tournament, their concentration might be thrown by all this—no offense, Chet."

"None taken," Chet said. "But Pete'll have plenty of

competition from out-of-towners anyway. Remember the guy at the 'keeper' game who didn't wear a mask?"

"Yeah . . ." Joe said.

"That was Steve Vedder, a player from Jewel Ridge. He's won a lot of tournaments," Chet said. "There'll be good players from all over at this thing."

"If we don't hear anything more, we'll call Con after school," Frank said, "and see what he found out."

"I'd still like to talk to Gerry again if we can corner him," Joe said. "That guy seems as slippery as an eel."

"He wriggled out of that fix at the mini-mall easily enough," Iola added.

"If we can track him down," Chet said, "I might even buy some cards from him."

"Chet!" Callie and Iola said simultaneously, disapproval in their voices.

Chet shrugged. "Hey, I've got a tournament to win, remember?"

After dinner the five of them regrouped at the Hardys' house. No one had seen Gerry during the day, and Chet told the others that he'd heard Gerry had called in sick.

"It's a bad time for him to be sick, considering how high the demand for cards is likely to be today and tomorrow," he said.

"Maybe he knew the police were going to be poking around and he didn't want to be any part of it," Iola said.

Frank shrugged. "There's no use speculating," he

said. "We'll just have to catch up with Gerry when we can."

"Did you find anything out from the police?" Callie asked.

"Con said they'd released Tim," Joe said. "They didn't find any other stolen cards in his locker. Good thing he had a receipt for that Coyote in his deck."

"What about my card, though?" Chet asked.

"Con said you could pick it up anytime," Frank replied.

"Well, what are we sitting around here for then?" Chet asked. "Let's go get it!"

The weather changed before Tuesday morning. Cold winds blew down from the northeast. Light coats and motorcycles disappeared in favor of winter jackets and cars.

Tension ran high during the school day. Tim returned to class, but didn't talk to anyone. Daphne orbited a sulky world of her own. Pete regarded everyone suspiciously. Even Chet seemed on edge.

The gamers talked in hushed whispers about that night's tournament. Gerry did a brisk business buying and selling cards before and after school, setting up in a park a block from the building. He wouldn't make time to talk with the Hardys, but Chet managed to buy a card or two from him.

"Boy," Joe said to Frank at the end of the day, "this game sure is making people paranoid."

* * *

The brothers hooked up with Chet and their girl-friends an hour before the start of the tournament; they all went down to the Sullivan Hotel ballroom together.

The venue was large, with more than thirty big tables arranged around the room. Chandeliers hung from the ceiling, suffusing the room with warm light. Gamers jammed the ballroom. Most of the players were nervously fingering through their decks one final time.

A podium stood on top of a low platform at one end of the hall. A group of older people chatted quietly near the stage. The Hardys recognized Dungeon Guild owner, Ron Felix, among the crowd.

"Wow!" Chet said, pointing at the platform. "See that guy? He's Troy King—the game's inventor." He indicated a skinny, bearded fellow with wire-rim glasses and frizzy reddish hair. "He'll be handing out the top prizes."

The tournament organizers gathered all the gamers into one corner of the room and began to group them for play. Joe, Frank, Callie, and Iola waited until Chet had been seated, and then found a good spot from which to watch him.

At seven o'clock, the tournament moderator—a slim woman with short black hair—called the hall to silence. "Noble Lords and Ladies," she said, "welcome to the Bayport Creature Cards tournament!" The audience exploded with applause.

The woman raised a hand for silence and continued, "Tonight we find out who is the supreme Creature Commander in Bayport and environs. The winner of this tournament will receive a crown trophy, and be declared Creature Commander King for this area!" Again, thunderous applause.

"In addition," she said, "our sponsors—including the Dungeon Guild, Sullivan Hotel, and the Kiff and Kendall restaurant chain—have provided generous prize packages for all the finalists. Now I'd like to introduce the Ultimate Creature Commander himself, Troy King!" She stepped back from the podium as Troy bounced up, all smiles.

Troy waited for the applause to die down, then he pulled out a small, Lucite container from behind his back. "You see before you," he said gravely, "the ultimate goal of every Creature Commander here—a Bone Leviathan card. It has an attack of ten, a defense of eight, and is immune to most magic."

The crowd let out an appreciative, "Ooh!"

"This card is being given out only to tournament winners," Troy continued. "And only this year. If you have what it takes, this Bone Leviathan could be yours. Now let the battles begin!"

With that, the game referees started the card playing at each table. Chet, Tim, Pete, Daphne, and Steve Vedder all made it through the first round, easily surviving the large battles set up at each table.

The groups got smaller in the second round. Tim got knocked out there, but the rest of them advanced.

At a break between rounds, Chet confessed that he

was hanging on by the skin of his teeth. "If only I had my old deck back," he moaned. The Hardys, Iola, and Callie urged Chet on. "We know you can do it," Iola said.

The third round featured three-person match-ups. Chet found himself competing against Daphne and Pete. The game was tense, with each of them jockeying for position—alternately attacking and supporting each other. As the game drew on, Chet began to lose ground. Sweat beaded on his forehead, and he frequently glanced at the gallery where his friends were sitting, looking for encouragement.

"I wish we could do something," Callie whispered to Frank.

"I wish we'd found his deck," Frank said glumly.

With their playing hands depleted, each contestant began a final push. Daphne laid out a Titanium Titan. Pete responded with a Bargeist.

Chet's eyes narrowed and he glanced from the card to Pete's impassive face. Chet played an Emerald Enchanter—which allowed him to simultaneously bring his Fiery Phoenix into play. The move kept him in the game for another turn, barely.

Daphne nodded her head admiringly at the play. She checked the cards in her hand for a moment, then brought out her Cobalt Bishop—a powerful anti-magic card.

Pete thought for a minute, then said, "This'll mess up all those spells you guys are using. Read 'em and weep, kiddies."

He placed the Coyote into his Creature army.

The crowd applauded Pete's move.

Chet went white. His eyes fastened onto the ketchup-stained corner of the card. He looked at Pete, who grinned back at him.

"That's my card!" Chet bellowed.

13 Accusations and Discoveries

"So you're the one who stole it!" Chet accused Pete, his face red with rage.

"You're crazy, Morton," Pete sneered. "Certifiably crazy."

The Hardys stood up, but before they could push through the crowd, Chet lunged across the table and tackled Pete.

Daphne grabbed her cards and cleared out as Chet and Pete tussled. They knocked over the table, and cards flew everywhere. The two of them rolled around the floor, wrestling.

Frank and Joe rushed forward, with Iola and Callie close on their heels. They dragged Chet and Pete apart just moments before tournament security arrived.

"Morton, you dope!" Pete shouted angrily.

"Thief!" Chet growled.

"Break it up! Both of you come with me. Now!" The security officer, a tall beefy man named Crawford, laid one big hand on Chet's shoulders and another on Pete's, and led them from the room. The Hardys and their girlfriends followed Chet out.

As they left, Ron Felix stepped up to the microphone at the front of the room. "Sorry for the disturbance, folks, but you can all get back to your games. Per the rules, both those players are disqualified. The tournament, however, will continue!" The crowd applauded and the noise from the disruption soon died away.

The security officer held Chet and Pete in the hotel office until the police arrived and took them to the Bayport PD. The Hardys drove their van to the station; Callie and Iola tagged along in Chet's car.

It took three-quarters of an hour before the brothers could get anyone to talk with them. Finally they spoke to Officer Chisholm, whom they'd met the previous morning.

"I wouldn't worry about this too much," she said to the teens. "Security guards bring kids down here mostly to scare them. Big tournaments like this don't like the bad publicity an arrest would bring. They rarely press charges unless someone gets hurt or something's broken. Your friend is lucky the fight didn't go further. Con Riley told me that all of you were okay—even this Morton character. Why'd this happen?"

"Chet thought that Pete stole his cards," Iola said.

"We're checking into that," the officer said, "but—right now—it looks like your brother made a mistake."

"What about the cards themselves?" Joe asked.

"We've got them," Officer Chisholm replied, "though we'll probably release them when we let Morton and the Kaufmann kid go—assuming we can sort the cards out that quickly."

"You said earlier that Chet was mistaken about the card being his," Frank said. "How can you be so sure?"

"The stain that Morton said was ketchup turned out to be a printer's error," the officer said. "We examined it with a good magnifying glass, and you can see the printing dots in the red stain. That red blotch is *printed* on the card."

"That's an odd coincidence," Joe said, "since Chet's stolen deck contained a stained Coyote card."

Officer Chisholm shrugged. "Life is full of odd coincidences. They make police work harder than it ought to be."

"Could you make us a photocopy of that Coyote card?" Frank asked.

"I don't see why not," Chisholm said. "I'll have our public assistant do it for you. Now, if you'll excuse me, I have to do the paperwork for Morton's release."

Twenty minutes later the PA brought Frank the photocopy he'd requested. Ten minutes after that, a forlorn Chet Morton met the group in the foyer.

"Did you get your cards back?" Iola asked.

Chet nodded. "Yeah, but not the cards Pete stole."

"Chet," Frank said, "Officer Chisholm assured us that the stain on the Coyote card was a printing error."

"I don't believe it," Chet said. "The stain was *exactly* the same as the one on my card. If Pete has that card, he's got to have the rest of my deck somewhere. The police should search his house."

"Chet, don't make a fuss," Iola said. "Let's get out of here before they change their minds about holding you."

Chet nodded and the five of them headed out the door. They went back to Chet's house, where Mr. and Mrs. Morton were waiting to speak with Chet and Iola. Not wanting to get into the middle of a family discussion, the Hardys and Callie agreed to meet Chet and Iola before school the next morning.

"Before we go, though," Frank said to Chet, "could we borrow your cards?"

"We promise to bring them back in perfect condition," Joe added.

"That'd be great," Chet said, "because they're looking pretty beat up right now. If you could bring them back *perfect*, I'd be grateful." He handed the deck to Frank, and the brothers and Callie went back to the Hardys' house, where Callie had left her car.

"Why'd you need Chet's deck?" Callie asked as they arrived.

"I wanted to check something," Frank said.

Callie crinkled her nose at him. "Don't be obscure,

Frank Hardy," she said. "What are you looking for?"

"I think Frank wants to check the stain on the photocopy Officer Chisholm gave us against the stain on Chet's White Knight card," Joe said.

"Right," Frank said. "Chet said that the two cards got stained with ketchup at the same time along their edges. I want to see if the stains match up."

"What will it prove if the stains match?"

"I'd rather not speculate until we've looked at the cards," Frank said.

"Well, if you think I'm going home before you check it out, you're crazy," Callie said. "Let's go."

The three of them went into the Hardys' kitchen. Joe fetched some sodas while Frank riffled through the deck, looking for the White Knight.

When he found it, he laid the card on the table and placed the photocopy next to it. Then he carefully matched the two stains up like pieces of a puzzle.

"They fit!" Callie said. "But how can that be? Why would a printer's error match the stain on Chet's card so exactly?"

"There's only one explanation I can think of," Joe said. "Counterfeiting."

"You mean somebody's making *fake* Creature Cards?" Callie asked.

"Why not?" Joe replied. "Chet said that the cards were like printing money for the company that sells them. It makes sense that crooks would want to cash in as well."

Frank nodded thoughtfully. "It could be that the

card thefts are just obscuring the larger crime. I think the thieves are reproducing the valuable cards—like the Coyote—and then selling the reproductions to unsuspecting kids."

"It's a great scheme," Callie agreed. "But how can you prove all this? I don't think the photocopy the police gave you will stand up as evidence. And who's doing the counterfeiting?"

"We don't know—yet," Frank said. "Maybe Pete's behind the whole thing. Stealing other players' cards would both eliminate competition and give him a greater pool of rare cards. Counterfeiting would also give him extra money, allowing him access to even more cards."

"Or maybe he's just greedy," Joe suggested. "In any case, planting a stolen card in Tim's locker would cut down on Pete's competitors. Plus, since Pete had a copy of the Bargeist anyway, planting Chet's to frame Tim wouldn't be any disadvantage."

"Pete seems like a pretty good suspect," Callie said.

"But he'd need a lot of gall to play the stolen cards against Chet," Frank said. "Plus, we could say the same about any of the other players, like Daphne, or the folks who just sell the cards, like Gerry or Ron Felix. Tim's not in the clear, either. With so many people trading and selling cards, it wouldn't take long for counterfeits to infiltrate the whole gaming community. That could make the culprit really difficult to track down."

"Boy, this whole scheme really burns me up," Joe

said. "Kids pay a lot for cards, then have them stolen, then pay again to replace them. Except, the replacements they're paying for may be counterfeits. It's a huge rip-off!"

"That's why we're going to stop this crook," Frank said. "It's too late to do anything more tonight, but starting tomorrow, we're going to bring that counterfeiter's house of cards down around his ears!"

14 Following Twisted Trails

The five friends met early Wednesday morning in the school parking lot. The Hardys filled Chet and Iola in on their deductions.

"We might be able to break this case, but we're going to need some cooperation from Pete to do it," Frank said.

"What do you mean?" Iola asked.

"So far," Joe said, "we're only speculating that Pete's Coyote is a counterfeit. The photocopy isn't good enough to prove anything. Plus, I want to look at his Bargeist, which we suspect might be a counterfeit as well."

"Joe and I looked at Chet's Bargeist with a magnifying glass last night after Callie went home," Frank said. "We found a number of minor scratches. If those scratches are printed on Pete's card, it would bear out

121

our counterfeiting theory. But we need to get a look at Pete's cards."

"What if Pete won't show you his cards?" Callie asked.

"Then it moves him up on our suspects list," Joe said.

Chet laughed ironically. "Good luck! After yesterday, I doubt that Pete'll want to talk to any of us."

"Maybe I could help there," Callie said. "Pete's sister, Lisa, is in some of my classes. I could try to arrange a truce."

"Great," Frank said. "If you can, Callie, let's meet at Pete's house this afternoon."

The school day passed with only a few minor incidents. Daphne walked around the halls glowing with pride; she'd placed second in the tournament, right behind Steve Vedder. She bandied the words "glorious combat" around as if she'd actually been in a war.

"She certainly came out on top in all this," Joe whispered to Frank.

"Yeah," the elder Hardy said. "I'm not sure she's our criminal, though."

Pete avoided any contact with the Hardys and Mortons, as did a number of other gamers who'd seen the fight. They all seemed to blame Chet. Sam Kestenberg sniped unceasingly at Chet and the Hardys over the incident.

Callie succeeded in her plan, though, and at the end of the day, she, Iola, Frank, and Joe all piled into the Hardys' van. Chet decided to take his own car, "In case I have to get out of there quick," he said.

They drove to Pete's house, which was in the older section of the Magus Hills subdivision. They made their way up to the spacious, two-story house where Pete and Lisa lived with their parents.

Pete answered the door, and his eyes narrowed when he took in who was there.

"I know I agreed to this meeting, but you've got a lot of nerve bringing Morton with you," Pete said angrily.

"I'm sorry I got us kicked out of the tournament," Chet said quietly.

"Sorry doesn't cut it," Pete replied. "I could have *won* that tournament."

"Calm down, Pete," Frank said. "We're all pretty ticked off about this whole affair. We think we know what's behind the trouble, but we need your cooperation to prove it."

"Cooperation, how?" Pete asked.

"We need to compare a couple of Chet's cards to yours," Joe said. "Specifically, the Bargeist and the Coyote."

Pete frowned suspiciously. "Why?"

"Joe and Frank think the cards are counterfeit," Iola blurted.

"Ha!" Pete scoffed. "That's the stupidest thing I've ever heard."

"Think about it a moment," Frank urged. "A counterfeiter could make a lot of money duplicating valuable cards—especially if he got to sell them back to people he'd stolen them from in the first place."

"Okay," Pete said. "I can accept that. You can come in. But if you're stringing me along . . ."

"Don't worry," Joe said. "We can prove what we say."

They adjourned to the Kaufmann dining room, and Pete fetched his deck. Chet and Pete pulled out the cards in question and examined them. Sure enough, Pete's Coyote matched the stain on Chet's White Knight. Plus, the tiny scratches on Chet's Bargeist had been faithfully reproduced on Pete's card.

"Counterfeit!" Pete gasped angrily. "I can't believe it! I can't believe those guys would rip me off!"

"Who ripped you off, Pete?" Joe asked. "Who'd you get those cards from?"

"The Black Knight got back in touch with me after I saw you guys on Saturday," Pete said. "He said there'd been a mix-up, apologized, and I bought the Bargeist from him the next night."

"And you still didn't recognize him?" Chet asked.

Pete scowled at Chet. "No. Like I told you before, he always wears a bulky motorcycle outfit."

"What about the Coyote?" Frank asked. "Who'd you get that from?"

"I got it from that little weasel Gerry Wise," Pete said. "I ought to go over there right now."

"I'll go with you," Chet offered. "Those guys *really* caused our trouble at the tournament."

"No," Joe said. "Frank and I will go talk to Gerry.

You keep out of it. Another incident could land both of you in jail—for real."

"But I can't just sit around," Chet complained.

"You don't have to," Frank said. "You and the girls go back to your house and get on the Net. We know the Black Knight's dealing bad cards. Check with his Web service provider, find out who runs that site."

"Right," Chet said, performing a mock salute.

"Joe and I will get in touch after we talk to Gerry," Frank concluded.

"Hey, you'll keep me in the loop on this, right?" Pete said. "I've got some big payback coming!"

"Don't worry," Joe said. "We'll let you know what happens."

While Chet, Iola, and Callie headed for the Mortons' home, Frank and Joe drove the short distance to Gerry's house.

Gerry smiled at the brothers when he answered the door.

"Hey, Hardy bros," he said, "what's up? Come on in." He led the brothers downstairs into the family room. Creature Cards lay strewn across a pool table in the center of the room. "Are you gonna get into the game?" Gerry asked.

"Not really," Frank said grimly.

"More like we've come to *raid* the game," Joe added.

Gerry's face fell. "What do you mean?" he asked.

"You've been selling people counterfeit Creature Cards, Gerry," Joe said. "That's not very nice."

Gerry shrugged, shook his head, and smiled again.

"I have no idea what you're talking about, man," he said.

"We're talking about people getting ripped off," Frank said. "About kids losing cards, money, and—in the case of Pete and Chet—getting disqualified from the Creature Cards tournament."

"As of this moment," Joe said, "all the evidence points to you. You set up the game where Daphne won Chet's stolen White Knight. You sold Pete the counterfeit Coyote. For all we know, you might even *be* the Black Knight."

"Whoa, man," Gerry said. "That's just too weird." Sweat began to bead on his forehead.

"The cops take a pretty dim view of robbery and counterfeiting," Joe said. "Our next step is to bring them in on this case, unless you can give us a good reason not to."

"I can't believe this," Gerry said. He held his forehead in his hands and began to pace the room. "It's like some nightmare. I didn't do anything wrong."

"Where'd you get the Coyote card you sold Pete?" Frank asked.

"I can't remember, man," Gerry said. "I get cards from a lot of places."

"Think," Joe urged.

"I get some cards over the Net, and some at conventions, and some from other kids at school," Gerry said, a note of panic creeping into his usually calm voice.

"Did you get any from the Black Knight?" Frank asked.

"No way," Gerry said. "I don't trust anyone whose face I can't see."

"So you've met him?" Joe asked, keeping the questions coming at a rapid clip.

"Once. But I got bad vibes from the dude," Gerry said.

"You could be lying," Frank countered. "Maybe *you're* the Black Knight. "We've seen you in a black jacket and motorcycle helmet."

"But the Knight's bigger than me, a lot bigger." Gerry's voice was almost pleading now.

"Then tell us where you got that card!" Joe said.

Gerry sank into a nearby sectional couch and closed his eyes. "It's too hard to remember," he said. "I've sold so many cards!"

"But this Coyote you sold in the last few days," Frank said, "and you had to have bought it since Chet's deck got stolen."

Gerry opened his eyes and looked up at the brothers. "I remember," he said.

"Who'd you get that card from?" Joe pressed.

"Sam Kestenberg," Gerry said. "I bought the Coyote from Sam Kestenberg."

15 The Black Knight Unmasked

Gerry collapsed back into the couch, exhausted.

"That doesn't make any sense," Joe said. "Kestenberg isn't interested in the game at all. He teases the players relentlessly."

"He told me that he sells the cards for his cousin, who needs to raise cash sometimes," Gerry said.

"Have you ever seen this cousin?" Joe asked.

Gerry shook his head. "Sam says he lives in Rhode Island and comes down to visit a couple of times a month."

"This is all starting to fall into place," Frank said. "Gerry, was Kestenberg the man who wore the demon mask to your game on Friday night?"

"I never saw that guy's face," Gerry said. "I told you that before."

Joe snapped his fingers. "Frank, it could have been

him. The guy in the mask was about the right size, and—now that I think of it—he hit me with a football shoulder block just before he took off." The younger Hardy rubbed his ribs at the memory. "Plus, Kestenberg rides a motorcycle. If I hadn't been so focused on the gamers as suspects, I would have remembered that long ago."

"Me, too," said Frank. He turned back to Gerry. "It looks like Kestenberg, the Black Knight, and the thief may be one and the same. But that doesn't let Gerry here off the hook."

"W-what do you mean?" Gerry asked nervously.

"Trafficking in stolen goods is still a crime," Frank said, "and Joe and I aren't convinced that you're not part of this scheme. You could be a vital part of the counterfeiting pipeline. At least, that's what the cops will probably think."

"I'm not," Gerry said, pleading. "Honest."

"Prove it," Joe said.

"How?" Gerry asked.

"Set up a buy with Kestenberg," Frank said. "Tell him that you have a client who needs some cards pronto. Say they're looking for the Coyote and the Bargeist. We'll set up our video camera at the meeting place. When Kestenberg passes you the counterfeit cards, we'll catch him in the act."

"Okay," Gerry said nervously. "When do you want to do this?"

"No time like the present," Joe said, smiling grimly. It took Gerry a half-hour to set up a meeting for nine o'clock that night. Not surprisingly, Kestenberg chose Old Bluff Road for the rendezvous. The brothers took Gerry with them and got their video camera from home. Then they went to Chet and Iola's house.

Iola met them at the door. "You'll never guess who runs the Black Knight site," she said.

"Sam Kestenberg," Joe replied nonchalantly.

Iola sounded crestfallen. "How did you know?"

"We're detectives, ma'am," Joe said in a fake western accent. "It's our job to know." He tipped an imaginary hat at her.

"Gerry told us that Kestenberg sells cards to him," Frank said. He took a few minutes to explain the situation and outline their plan.

"So, let's get him!" Iola said.

Frank shook his head. "The last time we tried to trap him, the Black Knight must have gotten there ahead of us and spotted us. Then, he called Pete to take the fall for him. This time, we have to get there even earlier and make sure we're not seen."

"We'll need all of you as backup," Joe said. "Chet, you, Iola, and Callie can come in your car. But you need to stay far enough away so that you're not seen."

"Let Iola drive my car," Chet said. "I *need* to be there when you bust Kestenberg."

"All right, Chet," Frank said. "You can come with us. Iola, you can park on the old utility road to the south of the meeting place. Kestenberg lives north of the bluff, so he'll probably arrive from the opposite

130

direction. We'll leave the van on the utility road, too, and hide the keys under the passenger seat. Callie can bring it when we call on the cell phone."

"Check," Iola said.

"Double check," echoed Callie.

"Good," Joe said. "Now Frank, Chet, and I better get going. Don't drop Gerry off too soon, Iola. And let him walk up the road to the meeting point so Kestenberg won't spot your car."

"Can I ride my bike up?" Gerry asked.

"It's a bit cold, but sure," Frank said. He turned to the girls. "Take Gerry home to get his bike."

Joe laid a hand on Gerry's shoulder and smiled. "Remember, Gerry, if you don't show up on your bike, we'll have the cops on your doorstep before midnight."

"I-I'll do my best, man," Gerry said. "I don't want to go to prison."

"Boy," Chet said as they drove out to Old Bluff Road, "I knew Kestenberg was a jerk, but I never would have believed he was behind this."

"We think he has a partner helping him," Frank said.

"Why would he need a partner?" Chet asked.

"Think about the equipment you'd need to make counterfeit Creature Cards," Joe said. "Especially ones that are good enough to fool most gamers."

"These counterfeits aren't something you could knock off on your PC at home," Frank said.

"Oh. I see," said Chet, though the expression on his face made it plain that he didn't have a clue what the brothers meant. "So, do you guys know who this partner is?"

"We've got some guesses, but no proof," Frank said.

"With luck," Joe added, "Kestenberg will confirm that hunch for us."

They reached Old Bluff Road, parked the car in their prearranged spot, and stowed the keys under the passenger seat. Then the three of them hiked through the woods up the hill to the meeting place.

The night was cold and dark, and they stumbled into tree branches more than a few times on their way. Despite that, they had their equipment set up within a half-hour. They cautiously scouted the area but saw no sign of Kestenberg. Then they called the girls to confirm that everything was going according to plan.

"What if Kestenberg doesn't show?" Chet asked, his teeth chattering from the cold.

"Then we'll have to find another way to turn his greed against him," Frank said.

Joe watched his breath billow into the night air like a tiny white cloud. "I think I liked the fog better," he whispered.

"Just wait," Frank said, "in a few weeks you'll be snowmobiling and loving every minute of it."

They sat quietly after that, waiting for Gerry and Kestenberg to arrive. Kestenberg got there first, dressed in his motorcycle helmet and leather jacket. He parked his motorcycle in the bushes on the side of the road, and then took a vantage point perilously close to where the Hardys and Chet were hiding.

Pretty soon Gerry came puffing up the road on his beat-up bicycle. When he neared the crest of the hill, he hopped off and walked up the slope with the bike.

Kestenberg stepped out from his hiding place.

"Hey, m-man," Gerry said, shaking slightly. "How's it going?"

"You tell me," Kestenberg said. "What's the matter, Gerry? Nervous?"

"N-no," Gerry said. "Just c-cold. You got the cards I wanted?"

"Yeah. I got them," Kestenberg said. He scanned the area but didn't spot the Hardys and Chet. Gerry's demeanor was clearly making him suspicious, though. "Did you bring the money?"

"G-got it right here," Gerry said. He reached into his pocket, but fumbled with the money as he took it out. The cash fell.

Gerry stooped to pick it up, but Kestenberg grabbed him by the collar and pulled him to his feet. "What's going on here, Gerry?" he asked. "First you ask to meet with me—which you've never done before—and then you act all nervous." He pulled Gerry up until they stood nearly eye to eye. "Is this some kind of set-up?"

Sweat began to pour down Gerry's head. "You shouldn't have made me your patsy in this counterfeiting scheme!" Gerry blurted.

Kestenberg's eyes narrowed. "I don't know what you're talking about," he said coldly.

"You sold me phony cards just before the tournament," Gerry said, seeming almost brave for a moment. "Admit it!"

Kestenberg decked him.

Gerry sprawled on the pavement, out cold.

Kestenberg stood over him and sneered. "Even if you tell anybody, wimp," he said, "there won't be any evidence."

16 The Secret Partner

Sam Kestenberg walked to where he'd hidden his motorcycle and got it out of the bushes.

Joe pulled out the cell phone and called Callie. "Gerry's out of the picture," he said. "Bring the van, quick!"

"Right!" Callie replied.

As the Hardys rushed down to help Gerry, they heard Kestenberg start his cycle and roar off. Seconds later Callie came zooming up the hill. Chet dragged Gerry off the road as she skidded the van to a stop. She flung open the door and hopped into the backseat. "Iola's right behind me," she said.

"I'll take care of Gerry until Iola gets here," Chet said.

Frank tossed Chet their cell phone and hopped in on the passenger side. "Call an ambulance for

Gerry," he called to Chet as Joe gunned the accelerator.

"What happened?" Callie asked breathlessly.

"Gerry folded under the pressure," Frank said.

"Can you catch Kestenberg?"

Joe shook his head. "He's probably got too big a lead. Fortunately, we have some idea of where he's going."

"Where?"

"Well, if he's smart," Frank said, "he'll head home and call his partner on the phone."

"Being Kestenberg, though, he'll probably go running to warn his buddy in person," Joe said.

"With luck, we can catch them both in the act," Frank said grimly.

"So," Callie said, looking from one brother to the other, "where are we going?"

They headed for Bayport's northwest side. When the Hardys were children, this part of town had been hills covered with scrub forests. In the last few years, however, industrial parks had sprung up where trees once grew.

"The key to this operation is *making* the cards," Frank said. "Kestenberg's good with his hands, but you need special equipment to make good counterfeits."

"The kind of equipment Bayport High doesn't have, but a print shop does," Joe said.

"It's a good thing Joe and I know the address of this particular print shop," Frank said.

Callie folded her arms over her chest and pouted slightly. "Well, clue me in whenever you're ready," she said.

The brothers merely smiled at each other.

The Hardys topped a denuded hill just in time to see Kestenberg entering a service driveway at the bottom of the small valley beyond. The counterfeiter pulled around to the loading dock of a large metal-sided industrial building. He got off his bike and went in the back door.

"Jackpot!" Frank said.

The sign in front of the building said, Coolcolor Quality Printing. Joe pulled the van around to the back of the building and parked behind Kestenberg's motorcycle. "Stay here and call the cops," Frank told Callie as he and Joe got out.

"What about you two?" Callie asked, trying to hide the concern in her voice.

"We've got to keep Kestenberg and his accomplice from destroying the evidence," Joe said.

"Good luck!" Callie called after them.

The brothers picked the lock on the back door and carefully sneaked inside the Coolcolor building. The door led onto a loading dock, piled high with pallets of promotional flyers, small magazines, and other printing jobs.

Beyond the stacked paper lay the main part of the building, a large room filled with printing presses. Some of them were tiny, suitable only for small, short run jobs. Dominating the room, though, was a huge web press—similar to the ones found in newspaper plants.

"Bet they use one of those small presses for the counterfeiting," Joe whispered.

Frank nodded. "They'd need something they could operate by themselves on nights or weekends."

None of the presses was running at the moment. The silence in the huge room was broken only by the sound of heated voices, drifting over from the big press.

"We should get rid of the plates and the film," Kestenberg said. "That way, they can't trace any of this back to us."

"You're crazy," said his accomplice. "We've spent a lot of time collecting those cards."

Frank and Joe recognized the other voice.

"Carl McCool," Frank whispered.

Joe nodded. "The part-time printing teacher."

"You sold the originals," McCool continued, "so we can't make new cards without the film. The plates are expendable, though. I've got acid here so we can re-etch them. No one will be able to tell what was on those plates. We'll hide the film in the storage unit where we've stashed the counterfeit cards. I rented that unit under an assumed name, so no one will connect it with either of us."

"That's a plan," Kestenberg said. "Where are the plates and film?"

"In the private safe in my office," McCool answered. "You can take the film to the storage unit while I erase the plates."

138

"Let's do it," Kestenberg said.

"We've got to keep them busy until the police show up," Joe whispered to Frank.

"You make sure that Kestenberg doesn't leave with the film," Frank replied. "I'll take care of McCool."

They split up and circled around either side of the big press. Joe took the shorter route. He came in sight of the office in time to see McCool hand a large, stiff envelope to Kestenberg. The crooks didn't see Joe, and he ducked back around the side of the press.

"What rotten luck," McCool growled. "First my scanning camera lens shatters on the Friday before that stupid tournament, then—after I 'borrow' a replacement from school, and smooth down the cops' feathers—this happens."

Kestenberg shrugged. "Those are the breaks. I'm going home after I drop these off," he said, brandishing the negatives. "In case Gerry calls the cops or something. I'll say I was just out riding if anyone asks."

"Right," McCool said. "Maybe you should skip school tomorrow, too—or at least skip my class. We don't want anyone connecting us."

"Yeah, okay," Kestenberg said. He ducked around the corner of the press and headed for the door. McCool walked toward a long, shallow etching pan under a hooded exhaust fan. A large chemical drum stood next to the old-fashioned etching station.

Frank rounded the corner of the big press just as

139

McCool placed his plates in the pan and reached for a gallon jug of acid. "You're not destroying those plates," the elder Hardy said.

McCool wheeled around, threw the jug at Frank, and charged. The elder Hardy ducked out of the way as the jug flew past, splattering acid. Fortunately, the corrosive liquid missed him.

McCool came at Frank like a rampaging bull. "You just made a fatal mistake, Hardy," McCool snarled, his face contorted in rage. He threw a punch at Frank's head.

Frank ducked out of the way and rammed his fist into McCool's stomach. It felt like hitting a wall. The printer spun and his elbow clipped Frank in the back of the head. Frank staggered and fell against the giant printing press. Smiling, McCool reached to a nearby steel pillar and pressed a large button marked Start.

"Going somewhere, Kestenberg?" Joe asked coolly. He stepped out in front of the exit door and folded his arms across his chest.

"Hardy!" Kestenberg snarled.

"Perceptive, as always," Joe said. "I think you and I have some unfinished business. Unless you'd rather just turn that film over to the police and give yourself up."

"Not in your lifetime, punk," Kestenberg said. He tossed the film to the floor and came at Joe with both fists.

Joe blocked Kestenberg's first punch and followed up with a smash to the jaw. Kestenberg reeled back but didn't go down.

Suddenly the room filled with thunderous noise as the big printing press sprang to life. The clamor distracted Joe momentarily and Kestenberg tagged him with a right cross to the chin.

Joe fell backward, stunned. Instead of fleeing out the unobstructed door, though, Kestenberg aimed a kick at the younger Hardy's head.

Frank lurched out of the way just as the huge press started up, barely avoiding being crushed between two big rollers. McCool came at him again, trying to push Frank back into the vast machine.

Frank jumped to his left, and McCool skidded on a puddle of spilled acid. He nearly fell but grabbed a steel support pillar and righted himself. Frank seized a nearby fire extinguisher and tossed it at the counterfeiter.

McCool caught the canister and heaved it back at Frank. The extinguisher missed Frank, but crashed into the drum of chemicals near the etching station.

The side of the drum staved in, and it fell over, spilling caustic liquid toward Frank and McCool. Frank hopped aside, but McCool leaped after him. The printer seized Frank by the throat and squeezed.

Joe grabbed Kestenberg's foot just before the thief's boot hit him in the head. He twisted and shoved upward. Kestenberg toppled backward into a tall stack of magazines atop a shipping pallet.

Kestenberg grabbed the side of the stack and heaved them at Joe. The magazines tumbled like a paper avalanche. Joe raised his arms over his head to protect himself from the cascade. Kestenberg charged forward, lowering his shoulder just as he'd done in Benson Mini-Mall.

This time, though, Joe was ready for him. He'd played more football than Kestenberg had and knew all the moves. At the last second Joe spun aside. He grabbed Kestenberg by the leather jacket and redirected the force of the thief's charge. Kestenberg crashed into a steel pillar and collapsed to the floor, unconscious.

Joe used Kestenberg's own belt to tie up the thief. Then he ran to help Frank.

Frank forcefully brought his arms up inside McCool's elbows, breaking the chokehold. McCool tried to head butt the elder Hardy, but Frank turned aside and the blow caught only his shoulder. He slammed his fist into McCool's neck and backed away quickly, putting the large corrosive puddle between them once more.

McCool winced in pain. He spotted the fire extinguisher near his feet and picked it up to heave it at Frank again. But the acid had weakened the canister. It burst as McCool lifted it over his head. A white cloud of CO_2 billowed out over the counterfeiter, blinding him.

Frank leaped over the puddle and punched McCool squarely in the jaw. McCool staggered back toward the huge press. Before he could fall between the rollers, though, Frank grabbed the front of the counterfeiter's shirt.

He punched McCool in the face once more, and the counterfeiter slumped, unconscious, to the floor.

"Wow," Joe said as he rounded the corner of the big press. "I thought you might need some help. McCool's built like a pro wrestler."

"Good thing this match was two out of three falls," Frank said.

Joe clapped his brother on the shoulder and said, "Frank Hardy, winner and still champeen!"

The sound of police sirens outside the printing plant brought weary smiles to the faces of both brothers.

After school the next day, the Hardys, Callie, Tim, and Daphne gathered at the Morton house. Iola Morton brought a tray of hot chocolate, chips, and sandwiches into the living room and set it on the coffee table.

"Dig in," she said. "You guys deserve it—not that I didn't help, you understand."

"You were great, Iola," Joe said as he sat down on the couch beside her. He gave her hand a friendly squeeze.

"I can't believe that Mr. McCool was behind the whole thing," Daphne said, ruffling her short red hair.

She picked up a mug of chocolate and took a swig.

"We knew that Kestenberg couldn't be the brains of this scheme," Joe said. "McCool was the only one who fit all the requirements for the counterfeiting mastermind."

"As a printer, he could produce the counterfeit cards on one of his small presses after his workers had gone home. Plus, his part-time job at school gave him access to the keys he needed to help Kestenberg steal cards from Daphne's locker, Mr. Pane's desk, and other places."

"What a rotten thing to do!" Callie said. She leaned across the coffee table and got herself a sandwich. "Getting fired and going to jail are too good for him!"

"They'll have to do, though," Frank said. "At least he and Kestenberg will be out of circulation for a long time. Creature Card officials can start getting the fake cards out of tournament play, too. I imagine it will take the police a while to figure out which cards belong to whom and who needs to get reimbursed for the crimes, though." He picked up a mug of cocoa and sighed. "I'm sure that Kestenberg and McCool resold a lot of those cards, too—either in person or over the Net. They're probably gone for good."

"So Kestenberg put Chet's Bargeist in my locker?" Tim asked.

"Yeah," Joe said. "He wanted to create a diversion and stir things up. Kestenberg did the legwork because McCool was too careful to do any of it himself.

As a teacher, he'd have been pretty conspicuous lurking around in the school corridors."

"Whereas, lurking was Kestenberg's modus operandi," Iola said. All of them laughed.

"Do you think you'll get your cards back, Daphne?" Callie asked.

Daphne took a sip of her drink. "I hope so," she said. "But if I don't . . . Well, I got a lot of the replacements I needed from Ron Felix, anyway."

"So that was you we saw buying cards in the waterfront park last Thursday night. You were the skull-masked player at Gerry's game, too, weren't you?" Joe said.

Daphne shrugged. "I might as well 'fess up," she said. "The tournament's over anyway, so there's no need to keep it secret any longer. You guys nearly caught me during Friday's cycle chase, too. If I hadn't known about that bridge . . ."

"Too bad Kestenberg eluded us that night," Joe said. "He must have taken a secret way out of those hills after he dumped his demon mask. We were left chasing you and Gerry."

"McCool and Kestenberg's plan was good," Frank said. "Lucky for us that they were in a rush to get their fake cards on the market. When the shop's lens broke and they had to borrow the school's, it put extra pressure on them. They got careless and didn't notice the small stain on Chet's White Knight and Coyote cards." He smiled. "Without Chet's love of ketchup, we might never have tumbled to their scheme."

Joe nodded. "The thefts kept all the gamers too paranoid to cooperate with each other. Plus, Gerry was a perfect fall guy in case anyone tumbled to Kestenberg's thefts. Gerry didn't know anything about the counterfeiting, but Kestenberg used him to pass along stolen and phony cards."

"Too bad Gerry wasn't paying more attention," Callie said. "These crimes might have stopped a lot sooner if he had been."

"Is he still in the hospital?" Iola asked.

"No, they released him this morning," Joe said. "Kestenberg didn't hurt him too badly. He took the day off from school, though."

"Who can blame him?" said Daphne. "There are a lot of gamers with counterfeit cards because of him. He might want to hide out for the rest of the semester."

"Speaking of hiding out," Callie said. "Where's Chet?"

"He had a phone call," Iola replied. "He said it was important."

Just then Chet came dashing into the room, a broad smile creasing his freckled face. "Guess what?" he said breathlessly.

"What?" the others replied in unison.

"I just got off the phone with Troy King from Creature Cards," Chet said. "As thanks for helping break up the counterfeiting ring, he's sending me and Pete our own Bone Leviathan cards—the same card they gave out as a prize at the tournament."

Daphne leaned her head back and said in mock

horror, "Argh. I can't stand it. Even when Chet loses, he wins!"

"I can't wait for the next tournament," Chet said. "Whether I get my old cards back or not, I should have a really killer deck by then."

"Chet," Joe said, "I'm all for your enthusiasm, but could you take it easier this time? Your last deck nearly got us all killed!"

Do your younger brothers and sisters want to read books like yours?

Let them know there are books just for *them*!

They can join Nancy Drew and her best friends as they collect clues and solve mysteries in

T H E

N A N C Y   D R E W

N O T E B O O K S®

Starting with

#1 The Slumber Party Secret

#2 The Lost Locket

#3 The Secret Santa

#4 Bad Day for Ballet

AND

Meet up with suspense and mystery in The Hardy Boys® are: The Clues Brothers™

Starting with

#1 The Gross Ghost Mystery

#2 The Karate Clue

#3 First Day, Worst Day

#4 Jump Shot Detectives

A MINSTREL® BOOK

Published by Pocket Books

2324

BILL WALLACE

Award-winning author Bill Wallace brings you fun-filled
animal stories full of humor and exciting adventures.

A MINSTREL® BOOK
Published by Pocket Books